Nicole 'Dell
MAGNA
Interactive Fiction for Girls

© 2010 by Nicole O'Dell.

ISBN 978-1-60260-844-3

Cover images: girls: Hilary Helton/Monsoon Images/Photolibrary
store: Joe Schmelzer/The Image Banks/Getty

Published by Barbour Publishing, Inc., P.O. Box 719, Uhrichsville, Ohio 44683, www.barbourbooks.com

Our mission is to publish and distribute inspirational products offering exceptional value and biblical encouragement to the masses.

ecpa Member of the
Evangelical Christian
Publishers Association

Printed in the United States of America.

Bethany Press International, Bloomington, MN 55438; February 2010; D10002230

Nicole O'Dell

MAGNA

Interactive Fiction for Girls

BARBOUR
PUBLISHING

DEDICATION

*To my grandpa, Papaw. He was the best possible earthly example
of grace and unconditional love. "Anything for my kids."
He said it. . .he meant it. . .he lived it.
I love you, Papaw. See you soon.*

Chapter 1

CLASS-ACT WARDROBE

"Purple and yellow polyester gym clothes? This school needs a new wardrobe!" Molly looked at the locker room mirror in disgust as she pulled her shirt off. "They're so ugly, and we have to wear them every single day."

"Plus, it's so gross that they only let us take them home once a week to wash them." Jess wrinkled her nose and pinched it with the tips of her fingers. She dropped the sweaty gym uniform into her duffel bag, careful to touch as little of it as possible.

"I know." Sara gestured over her shoulder to an unkempt girl seated on the bench down the row. "*Some* people should wash their clothes a lot more often than that."

Molly looked at the girl—her clothes way too small and her hair obviously unwashed. *She has more pimples than I have freckles. But still, why does Sara have to be mean?* Molly turned away to swipe some gloss on her lips and changed the subject. "Forget about gym clothes for a sec. What about the rest of our clothes? You know, we're in high school now. I don't know about you, but I'm having trouble finding cool stuff in my closet. Everything is so junior high." Her voice trailed off in a whine as she tied her long blond hair back in a ponytail and fluffed her bangs with her fingertips.

Sara nodded as she ran a brush through her dark, silky hair. "I kn–"

"I'm having the same—" Jess said at the same time and then laughed.

Molly zipped her bag shut. "Okay. Well, I see we're all having the same problem then. We should do something about it."

"I've been thinking. . . . We need to get jobs." Jess slammed her locker closed and spun the combination lock.

"No way anyone would hire us. We're not old enough." Sara slipped into step with Molly and Jess as they walked out into the hallway and blended in with the student traffic.

"Besides, we're not trained for anything."
Molly shrugged, dismissing the issue.

Jess jumped in front of them and turned
in a half circle, walking backward. "Well, I've
thought of all of that, and I have solutions." She
grinned and put up her hand to stop the flood
of protests. "Just hear me out a sec. Okay?"

Molly closed her mouth and nodded,
then winked at Sara. Jess was taking charge.
Something interesting would happen whether
they wanted it to or not.

Sara scowled and shook her head, then she
sighed.

Jess grabbed their sleeves and pulled them
to a stop. "Okay, we need new clothes, so what
better place to work than a clothing store? On
top of a paycheck, we'd also get a discount." She
raised her eyebrows.

"Now that's a good point." Molly nodded.

"Hadn't thought of that, huh?" Jess teased.
"Sure, we're not sixteen, which makes it more
difficult to actually get the job. But we all get
good grades and have an impeccable school
record with lots of service activities and
extracurricular things."

"I don't know if that's enough." Sara's
eyes narrowed. "Lots of people have all that,

plus they're older—some even with work experience."

"I made some calls," Jess continued, unfazed. "Here in Wisconsin, all we need in order to get a job at fifteen is a work permit. We'll need permission from our parents and a letter of recommendation from the school principal and a few teachers."

"But why would a business want to hire us?" Molly asked when Jess stopped for air. "I mean, Sara's right: They could get an older girl with more experience and a later curfew."

Jess paused at the door to her math class and turned to face the girls. "They can get someone older than us, sure. But why would they? We're not attached at the hip to a boyfriend, we have nowhere else to be, and we're highly trainable because we don't have any bad habits yet." She entered her classroom without another word.

Molly and Sara looked at each other and chuckled. They shook their heads as they walked away. They would probably be getting jobs—Jess would see to it.

"I do like the idea of a discount," Molly admitted. "More bang for the buck."

"I just hope we can work at the same place, at the same time." Sara brushed her hair out of her eyes. "I'd hate to have a job with no one I know to work with."

Molly snorted. "Oh no! I feel sorry for anyone who hires the three of us together!"

"Let's make a list!" Molly jumped onto Sara's fluffy pink bed, crossed her legs, and poised her pen to write. "Where do we want to work?"

"Claire's—good jewelry." Sara touched the silver hearts dangling from her ears.

"Old Navy—great jeans," Jess added.

"What about a department store?" Molly tapped the tip of the pen on her chin. "I mean, think about it. Everything we could ever need would be in that one store."

"Yeah, but those stores are so big we might have to work in different areas."

"That's true, but a big store like that might be the only place that has three spots to fill at the same time," Jess countered.

"I've got it! Come here." Sara jumped up and scampered to her older sister's room with Molly and Jess close at her heels. She ran right to the overstuffed closet. "This." Sara pulled out a cute sweater. "These." She grabbed three great shirts and started to pile the things on the bed.

"These!" Sara showed them girls the coolest pair of jeans ever.

"I get it. Your sister has great clothes. So what?" Jess rolled her eyes.

"What do these clothes all have in common?" Sara looked from one to the other, waiting for an answer.

Molly stared at the clothes and tapped her lip with her finger. Then it hit her. "Magna." She grinned. "They're all from Magna."

"Right! That's where we need to work." Sara gave one confident nod.

Molly watched as smiles spread across their faces.

Perfect! Molly fingered the clothing. Magna, the most popular clothing store among the older girls, was the perfect place for them to get jobs. But now that they knew *where* to get jobs, they needed to figure out *how* to get jobs.

"Get out that trusty paper of yours, Molly." Jess turned on her heel and led the way back to Sara's room. "We need to plan. Let's make a list of what we need to do."

"We need to get our parents' permission; otherwise nothing else matters," Molly reminded them. "That might be a deal breaker for me."

"True. Put that at the top of the list," Sara said. "Then, we need letters of recommendation."

They brainstormed, schemed, and planned for over two hours about how to get their dream jobs.

1. *Get a letter of permission from parents.*
2. *Get letters of recommendation from the principal and at least one teacher.*
3. *Figure out hours available to work.*
4. *Get a ride to the mall.*
5. *Pick up applications.*
6. *Fill out applications and turn in to the store manager.*
7. *Find a really cool outfit to wear to the interview.*
8. ~~*Find three other places to apply for jobs, just in case.*~~
9. *Find someone to teach us about interviewing.*
10. *Find out how much of a discount there is!*

"About number eight, I hope we're not sorry we decided not to look at other places." Molly shook her head. It couldn't be wise to limit their options so much.

"We can always make adjustments if things don't work out." Jess unfolded her long body and stretched her arms high above her head. She rolled a curl between her fingers.

"Yeah, I think we've got a good plan." Sara's eyes brightened when the garage door opened. "In fact, I'll go talk to Mom as soon as you two are gone. A single mom of two teenage girls is never going to mind the idea of one of them getting a part-time job."

"What about you, Jess?" Molly chuckled. "Do you even have to ask your parents?"

"Of course I'll have to ask. But they won't care." Jess shrugged. "Mom and Dad don't say no to much."

"Well, I might have a problem." *No way they'll go for it.* Molly chuckled. *I'll have to be very careful how I ask.* "We'll see. For now, though, we'd better go. My mom is probably waiting for us outside."

"This is a wonderful dinner, Kay. Will you please pass me the potatoes?" Molly's dad rubbed his trim stomach.

"You're awfully quiet tonight, Molly. Something wrong?" Mom peered intently at her.

Uh-oh. This isn't how I wanted to bring this up. She sat up a little straighter. "No, not at all." Molly smiled and took the bowl of potatoes to pass on to her dad. "I'm just thinking about something—nothing bad, though." *Oops. Looked like Mom wasn't buying it.*

Mom pressed a little harder. "Why don't you run whatever it is by me and your dad? I'm sure we can help."

Better tell her before she gets too worried and assumes the worst. Molly tried to sound confident. "Well, it's just that Sara, Jess, and I are thinking that we might want to get jobs. The thing is, we obviously need our parents' permission. I'm just thinking about the best way to go about getting that." She took a forkful of meat loaf and rolled it in her puddle of ketchup, hoping to look casual.

Mom pulled her head back like she'd been slapped. Her eyes open wide, she said, "Wow, this came out of nowhere. Hmm. Well, you're going to have to give us a little time to talk about this."

Molly's dad held up one finger.

Antsy, she poked at her food while she waited for him to finish the bite he'd just forked into his mouth.

For the next fifteen minutes he peppered her with questions about where she wanted to work, how much she wanted to work, how she'd schedule everything important in her life without letting school or church suffer, and most importantly he wanted to know why she wanted a job.

Molly squirmed. Her answer would sway their decision one way or another. She couldn't just say she wanted money for clothes. They'd never go for that. Oh, they might offer to buy her a new outfit, but that would be it. Somehow, without lying, she'd have to come up with the perfect answer.

"Well, there's more than one reason." Elbows on the dining room table, Molly ticked off the reasons on her fingers. "A job looks good on my transcripts. Working would be a really good experience for me. It will give me extra spending money for activities, clothes, and other stuff that comes up. I can help you guys with my expenses—"

"I'm not sure I'm liking the sound of this so far, Molly." Mom's worry wrinkles knit together between her brows. "Your dad and I have no problem paying for the things you need—and even a few wants every now and then. I don't know if I like the idea of you having a job now. You'll be working the rest of your life. Why start now?"

Don't sound whiny. "The thing is. . .I don't do much. I go to school and church, and I hang out with my friends. Why not hang out with my friends at a job? I have the time, and it's better to spend my time that way than to just shuffle around the mall aimlessly. . .isn't it?"

"In theory, yes." Her dad nodded. "It's not the working itself that's the problem. It's the commitment to the job and what that will require from you. Your mom and I are going to need to talk about this. We're not saying no. Just give us a chance to talk."

Molly opened her mouth to argue but had second thoughts. "Sure, Dad. Thanks for thinking about it." She stacked the dinner plates and headed off to the kitchen to wash them.

Several times she thought of ways to make her case stronger and turned to run back in to make her argument, but she refrained. Some things were better left alone.

A few hours later, Molly put her math book down and rubbed the creases from her forehead just as she heard a knock at her door. "Come on in."

The door opened, and Mom and Dad both entered her bedroom.

"Whoa. To what do I owe the pleasure of both of you coming to my room?" *Look like it's a no.*

"Your mom and I have reached a decision, and

we want to talk to you about it." Dad pulled up her desk chair and sat backward on the seat. His red tie draped over the backrest in front of him.

Mom sat down on the edge of the bed, bouncing Molly's book to the floor with a thud. No one bent to pick it up.

The suspense is killing me.

"Well, we don't really think it's going to be easy to find one, but if you're serious about wanting to—"

Molly's eyes grew wide and expectant, her heart double-timing.

"—we'll let you get a job. After all, the early bird catches the worm."

"Reeeally? Are you serious?" Molly slapped her legs and jumped off the bed. She ran to her dad and threw her arms around his neck. "Thanks, Dad!" She gave her mom a huge hug, too. "Thanks, Mom."

"Hold on, before you get too excited." Her mom's expression was very serious. "You have to agree to a few things first, Moll." *Splash!* Mom threw a bucket of cold water on the excitement.

"A few things? Like what?" Did she really want to know?

Mom looked at Molly. "Now, don't get all defensive. These are just some basics you should expect anyway." She looked at Dad as if asking him to take over.

"You're going to need to keep your grades up. You'll have to stay as involved at church as you are now—no skipping youth group for work and no working on Sundays at all so we can go to church together."

Molly cringed. "Youth group—I totally agree. But Sundays?" She tipped her head and stuck out her bottom lip.

"Just because you think it's boring to sit in church with us doesn't mean we're going to cave, Moll. We've had this talk before." Mom lifted her chin and crossed her arms.

Oops! Now's not the time to cause a problem. "No big deal. I didn't want to work on Sundays anyway—because of God, not church."

"God is everywhere, every moment. Sunday mornings, we're in church. Period." Dad continued after a slight pause. "You can only work two weeknights and one weekend shift. No more. And we get final approval on the type of job you get." He raised one eyebrow in a question mark and looked at Molly.

"That's it?" Molly breathed a sigh of relief. "No problem. I pretty much expected those rules anyway."

"Well, okay then." Mom smiled. "As long as

we're clear on those things, you can go ahead and try to find a job somewhere like the mall, but I don't want you working at a restaurant." She rose to leave the room, and Dad followed.

"Wish me luck," Molly called after them as they pulled the door shut. *I'm going to need it.*

Chapter 2

HELP WANTED

"Check your watches, girls. You have an hour and a half to collect applications. If you use your time wisely, you may even be able to fill them out and turn them in before I pick you up." Molly's mom inched the car up to the side of the curb in front of the main mall entrance to drop off Molly, Sara, and Jess after school on Tuesday—during the mall's slowest hours—so they could go job shopping.

"It won't take even that long, Mrs. Jacobs. We only want to apply at Magna. So we're going to go right there." Jess got out of the car first. "We should be able to fill out our applications and be back here to meet you in plenty of time."

"Really?" She looked surprised. "I hope you realize that by only applying at one place, you severely limit your chances of actually getting hired." She smiled and shook her head.

Sara and Molly climbed out of the car next, careful not to wrinkle their clothes or mess up their hair. They each took a moment to look in the side-view mirror before they headed for the entrance. Jess took a quick peek at her clear complexion and no-fuss curly hairdo, and Sara smoothed her dark flyaways.

Molly tousled her straight blond bangs so they wouldn't look so blunt. One last glance—makeup was fine. All set. They turned and waved good-bye to her mom. There it was, that familiar longing. She knew what Mom was thinking: *My little girl is growing up too fast.* Molly smiled and blew her mom a kiss before she turned to catch up with the others.

Sara and Molly stalled at the makeup counter in Macy's while Jess checked out the running shoes. They wasted at least thirty minutes.

Enough's enough. Molly took control. "Okay. We're either going to do this or we're not. What are we so nervous about anyway? I mean, you guys, it's not like we're doing anything wrong.

We're offering to work for them—not trying to steal clothes."

Sara and Jess nodded, their tense shoulders relaxing.

Molly looked in the mirror at the makeup counter and wiped at the edges of her lipstick. "We'll go together, walk right up to the manager, and one of us will do the talking. Ask for three applications—how hard could it be?"

"Okay, but who's going to do the talking? I don't think I can." Sara blanched.

"Oh, I'll do it if no one else will." Molly sighed. She spun toward the entrance to Magna and marched in.

Jess and Sara scrambled to catch up.

Passing the tables of folded screen-print T-shirts and hooded sweatshirts, racks of expensive jeans, and finally, toward the back, the clearance racks of shorts and flip-flops, Molly approached a woman with a scanner in her hands.

She looked important. Must be the manager. "Hi, I'm Molly Jacobs, and these are my friends Jess Stuart and Sara Thomkins. We'd like to know if you're hiring right now."

"Hi, Molly. I'm Donna." She nodded at Jess and Sara while she shook Molly's hand. "As a matter of fact, I do have some openings.

I had several girls leave for college in the past couple of weeks. Let me get you girls some applications." She bent down to get the pad of applications from under the cash counter. The girls grinned at each other.

"Here you are. Just fill them out and bring them back when you can." She shook Molly's hand again and nodded at Jess and Sara.

Jess reached out her hand to shake Donna's. "Thanks so much for your time."

Sara shook Donna's hand and smiled but said nothing.

Be calm. They walked out of the store as casually as they could. As soon as they entered the mall commons and turned the corner, out of the view of Magna's front entrance, Molly turned to the other two, grabbed their forearms and squealed, her feet doing a little dance.

Jess collapsed against the brick wall that divided two stores, and Sara fanned her face as though she were hyperventilating. So relieved to have the hardest part behind them, they dissolved into nervous giggles that gave way to laughter.

The girls slumped in their bus seats for their ride home from school on Friday afternoon. "I can't believe she hasn't called yet." Molly looked out the window. Sara was glum beside her.

"I'm sure we won't get a call over the weekend, because that's when the mall is the busiest," Jess added.

"My dad said we should call to check on our applications if we don't hear anything, so maybe we could do that on Monday." Molly stood up and held on to the seat in front of her when the bus stopped at the corner where she and Jess got off. Molly slipped off a wet step and held on to the door to avoid falling into the muddy puddle. Once she regained her footing and they were out of the way of the departing bus, they looked back to wave good-bye to Sara.

She mouthed through the rain-covered window, "Meet me online."

Molly and Jess nodded, pulled their hoods over their heads, and plodded through the cold, pouring rain. They hurried to their front doors, right across the street from each other, waved good-bye, and then disappeared into their homes. Molly stepped into her foyer and shook the rain off like a puppy. Small droplets hit the floor as she wriggled out of her hoodie.

"Hello?" The house seemed strangely quiet, like it stood alone all day. *Where's Mom?* Molly went into their newly remodeled kitchen. On the shiny granite countertop lay a note that read: *Sorry, I forgot to mention that I had my book club meeting and then a dentist appointment. I should be home by 5, Dad by 6. I'll bring dinner. Be good. Love you, Mom.*

Hmm. What to do? Sara's last words rang in her head: "Meet me online." *Perfect!* Molly foraged for a granola bar, a few cookies, and a soda. Her mom's voice counting the carbs echoed in her brain. She shook off the guilt, grabbed her junk food and, to make Mom happy, threw an apple on the pile. She scooted the desk chair up to the idle computer in the family room. Wiggling the mouse, she brought the screen to life. Jess had already logged on.

Molly: *Hey Stranger! Long time, no see.*

Jess: *HA, right. Sara should be here in a few.*

PRINCESSSARA123 HAS SIGNED IN.

Molly: *Speak of the devil lol*

Jess: *Princess Sara, when are you going to change your screen name?*

Sara: *I'm not! I've had this one for 5 yrs. It's staying.*

Molly: *Why do I feel like we've had this discussion before???*

Sara: *LOL*

Jess: *OK OK lol*

Molly: *Phone brb*

Annoyed, Molly stepped away from her computer to answer the phone on the end table next to the mahogany leather sofas. "Hello, Jacobs residence. Molly speaking." No way she'd keep saying that when she answered the phone after the job search ended.

"Hi there, Molly. It's Donna from Magna calling in reference to your job application."

Trying not to make any noise, Molly danced around for a moment. "Hi Donna. It's great to hear from you. What can I do for you?" She glanced at the computer screen—her friends were just talking nonsense. She stepped over and grinned, her fingers poised above the keyboard. *This will get them going.*

Molly: *MAGNA*

Jess: *Huh?*

Sara: *You mean on the phone? What is she saying?*

Jess: *Is it for an interview? Ask if she's going to call us!*

Molly turned away from the screen so she wouldn't be distracted.

". . .group interview. There'll be approximately six to seven girls in that

interview. It's pretty informal, just a way for
me to sort through some applicants. Are you
interested?"

"Oh, very much." *Woo-hoo!*

"Okay, great. Come to the store on Monday
at three o'clock. I'd imagine it will take no
longer than an hour. Do you have any other
questions?"

Should she ask about Sara and Jess?
Probably not. "I do have one question. How
many positions are you looking to fill?"

"I have two openings right now. It could
possibly be three, depending on hours and
availability. But we'll figure all of that out later.
So, I'll see you on Monday at three o'clock?"

"Definitely! Thank you so much for calling."
Molly placed the phone back in its cradle and
hurried back to her computer. She started
typing before she even sat down.

Molly: *Interview Monday at 3.*

Jess: *No way! What about us?*

Molly: *I don't know, she didn't say. Fingers
crossed.*

Sara: *That's so cool! What are you going to wear?*

Molly: *I don't know. . . . It's going to have to be
good though.*

Jess: *Phone brb.*

Molly: *Wouldn't that be cool if Donna called all three of us!?*

Sara: *I'll bet that's her on the phone with Jess right now.*

Jess: *MAGNA*

Sara: *Watch, I'll be the only one who doesn't get an interview! It would be because I didn't say a word when I met Donna. What a dummy!*

Molly opened her soda and took a big drink. She drummed her fingernails on the desk and took a bite of a cookie. What was taking Jess so long?

Sara: *YAWN*

Jess: *I'm back. Interview Monday at 3. It's a group interview.*

Molly: *Oh, right. I forgot to mention that part.*

Sara: *Hang on, phone*

Molly: *Ho hum. . .waiting. . .lol*

Jess: *I know! Come on already!*

Sara: *Monday at 3 pm. . .me, too!*

Molly: *Okay. Planning to do, girls. My house tomorrow morning at ten?*

Jess: *Hey, maybe your dad can help us practice for the interview.*

Molly: *Maybe. Garage door, gotta go. Bye!*

Molly shut down the instant message program and gathered up the remains of her snack.

"Hi, Moll. I'm home."

Molly met her mom in the kitchen as she came through the garage door. Mom set her purse, keys, and a few grocery bags on the kitchen counter.

Grabbing the milk and eggs, Molly went to the refrigerator. "So, guess who called this afternoon?"

Her mom paused to think for a second. "Hmm, the president of the United States?"

"No! Way better than that, Mom."

"I'm going to guess, then, that the manager from Magna called to set up an interview." Her eyes twinkled.

"Yep! How'd you guess?"

"She actually called me this morning. She wanted to talk to me about you and your responsibility level and to find out if your dad and I were supportive of you taking on a job. She appeared to be very impressed with how you handled yourself when you first met."

"Really?" Maybe she'd get the job after all. But what if she was the only one who did? "I wonder if she called Mrs. Thomkins and Mrs. Stuart, too."

"I'm not sure. She didn't say." Mom hesitated. "Can I give you a small piece of advice, dear?" When Molly nodded, she continued. "Just be sure to be your own person in that interview. You're going there as an individual, looking to fill an individual spot on a team. If you go there as a unit of three girls who can't function without each other, she won't think you'll do well alone. Do you get what I'm saying?"

"Oh yeah, Mom. I've already thought of that." Molly stood on the tips of her toes to put the crackers up on the top shelf.

"Let me ask you this then. If you get hired, but your friends don't, will you still want the job?" She leaned back against the counter and crossed her arms across her chest.

"I think so. But it wouldn't be as fun." She shrugged one shoulder. *What if? Hmm.* "I mean, we're doing this together. But if that's what happens, I still want to do it."

"Just be sure you know what you're getting into, honey."

Palms sweating, the three girls, along with four others—obviously older than they—waited outside Donna's office for ten minutes before their meeting. Molly nervously checked her watch and chuckled when she saw three others do the same. Sliding her hands down her stylishly faded jeans, she hoped her palms would be dry when she needed to shake Donna's hand.

Molly studied the four older girls. *Could they be just as nervous as I am?*

At exactly three o'clock, the door to Donna's office opened and she stepped out with a huge smile, looking like a layered and accessorized Magna mannequin. She shook each girl's hand and called them by name.

Good memory.

Donna invited them to follow her back into a huge storeroom. Molly tipped her head all the way back so she could gaze up at the floor-to-ceiling shelves full of stacks of jeans and rows of shoeboxes. Along the sides, racks were stuffed full of shirts and dresses ready to make their debut on the sales floor.

Molly looked around in amazement at all the hard work that went into preparing the store for success. Afraid Donna would think she'd been daydreaming, Molly gathered her thoughts, took her seat with the other girls, and forced herself to pay attention.

Nervous and wanting the job more than ever, Molly flubbed the answers to several of

Donna's first few questions. *Ugh.* Hopefully her
sincerity made up for her dumb answers. She'd
better get it together.

"What would you do if someone walked into
the store, picked up a T-shirt, walked directly
to you, and said, 'I want to buy this'?" Donna
hugged her clipboard to her chest and looked at
them expectantly.

Sara answered, "I'd ring her right up or find
someone who could, if I wasn't trained to do
that yet."

Jess took it a step further. "I'd offer her a
fitting room."

Megan, one of the other girls, said, "I'd ask
her if she had any coupons."

Donna tapped her lips with her pen and
nodded along with each answer. She seemed to
be waiting for something more.

Molly raised her hand about shoulder high
and spoke up. "I'd say something like, 'Great
choice! Come on, I'll help you find a necklace
and earrings to go with that.'"

"Aha! That's what I'm looking for, girls."
Donna beamed.

Finally a shining moment. Molly could
hardly contain herself.

"We're a sales team here at Magna."

Donna continued. "It's a fun place to be, but this company only exists because we sell to customers. Our business is built on selling complete looks, total wardrobes—not T-shirts. Does that make sense?"

Sara piped up, "But what if she only wants the T-shirt?"

"Ah." Donna pointed a finger. "See, that's the thing, Sara. Customers come into the store only wanting the T-shirt, but they leave our store grateful for the knowledgeable and helpful sales team who helped them discover what else they really needed."

After another half hour of open discussion, Donna said, "Girls, this has been a blast for me. I love eager young minds who want to learn and who are excited about this business. I hope you've gotten your questions answered. If you think of any others, feel free to call me here at the store anytime."

"Donna, if you don't mind me asking, when will you be making a decision?" Molly asked as they all stood to leave.

"Hmm, good question. I have a few more references to check and people to talk to. But I've got a pretty good idea of the direction I'm going to go." She looked at the schedule on top of the stack of papers she had in front of her. "I'll be in touch with each of you by Friday to let you know one way or another. Does that sound okay?"

"Mm-hmm." Sara nodded.

"Perfect." Jess grinned. "I'm looking forward to hearing from you."

Molly shook Donna's hand. "Sounds good, Donna. Thanks for your time and the opportunity."

Sara slapped herself on the forehead when they left the store. She put her head on Molly's shoulder as they walked along the storefronts in the mall. "I just know I totally blew it. Why couldn't I have at least shaken her hand? Not to mention my horrible answers." She shook her head and moaned. "Oh well. Nothing I can do about it now."

"You did fine!" Jess laughed. "Donna knows it was your first interview. Don't sweat it." She pointed out a cute top in a store window they were passing. "Although, Molly's got the job for sure."

"We'll see. I'm still hoping we all get offered a job."

"She'll never pick me. I can't even string two words together to make a sentence." Sara lifted her head and groaned again.

"What if only one of us gets hired?" Jess looked from Molly to Sara.

Molly stopped walking and turned to face them. "Or none—maybe no one will get the job." *Which would be worse?*

Chapter 3

A RISING STAR

"Look, if Donna had wanted to hire me, she would have done so already." Molly shook her head and threw the ball across her yard. "Go get it, Rocco!"

Her Brittany spaniel sprinted across her yard, rust-colored curls waving like flags.

Molly turned to Jess and Sara, whose lifeless forms were slumped in deck chairs. "I mean, it's been ten days. She had already checked my references and even spoke to my mom before the interview. There was nothing left for her to do." She sighed. "At least with you two, she hadn't done any of that yet, which could at least explain what's taking her so long."

"Nice theory." Jess smirked. "But you can't

spin the fact that she thought enough of you the first time she met you to do your reference checks even before the interview."

"And she still hasn't even called our parents." Rocco dropped the ball between Sara's feet. She picked it up and threw it.

"Well, it looks like it's not going to matter anyway. She hasn't contacted any of us." Molly lay back on the grass. "Rejection. Who knew it would sting so much?"

Jess sat up. "Maybe we should think about applying somewhere else."

"Maybe it's a sign that we shouldn't get jobs at all," Molly suggested.

The patio door slid open, and Mrs. Jacobs leaned her head out. "Molly, phone for you. Uh, you might want to come in here to take it."

Molly furrowed her eyebrows and threw the ball one more time, sending Rocco after it—a blur of fur darting across the grass—before she went to the house.

"Who is it, Mom?" Molly slid the door shut behind her.

Covering the receiver with her hand, Molly's mom whispered, "It's the manager from that store."

Molly wiped some doggy slobber on her jeans

and then grabbed the phone. She took a deep breath and waited for her racing heart to calm down before answering. "Hello, this is Molly."

"Hi Molly. It's Donna from Magna calling. I'm very pleased to be able to offer you a position with our store if you're still interested."

"I'm very interested! Thank you so much." Molly danced around and punched the air while trying to maintain her composure on the phone.

Donna skimmed the topics of hourly wage, start date, training, and a schedule. "We'll cover all of that in more detail during the training."

"That sounds great!" *What about Jess and Sara?*

"I'm really looking forward to having you start with us, Molly. Your training will begin on Monday. You'll be training alongside Amber. It's much easier to start you both at the same time. How does that sound?"

"Perfect. I can't wait." Molly grinned at her mom, who smiled and nodded. *No Jess and Sara, I guess.*

"Great. Do you have any other questions?"

"I don't think I have any. . ."

Mom pointed at her clothes and raised her eyebrows.

"Oh Donna, just one question. What should I wear for training?"

"The first week it won't matter that much, because you won't be on the sales floor very often. Casual, jeans and a nice top, something like that. After that you'll need to wear Magna merchandise. We'll talk about all of that in your training."

"Great. I'm really excited. Thanks so much, Donna." Molly hung up the phone and grabbed her mom's hands and jumped up and down. "I can't believe it!"

"Congratulations, dear. Your dad is going to be so proud of you."

Uh-oh! Molly looked out the window. She stood rooted to the spot and stared at her friends playing with her dog in the backyard, knowing they'd be disappointed. *Bittersweet.*

Holding the door handle, Molly turned toward her mom and opened her mouth to ask her what she should do about her Sara and Jess. But Molly already knew. She'd have to tell them right away. She shook her head and slid the door open. *Sigh.*

Sara and Jess compared cell phone pictures while Rocco barked for attention. Jess flipped hers shut when she saw Molly's face. "What happened? You look like you just lost your best friend."

"I may have, I guess."

"What are you talking about? What happened?" Sara slipped her phone into her bag.

"That was Donna on the phone." Molly looked down at her hands and picked at an invisible hangnail, dreading what she had to tell them next.

When she didn't speak right away, Sara raised her eyebrows and shrugged. "What did she say?"

Still not looking up, Molly said, "She offered me a job."

"Hey, that's great!" Jess grinned.

"And that doesn't mean she's not going to call us, too, right?" Sara asked hopefully. She looked at Jess. "Hey, maybe we should get home in case she does."

Still smiling, Jess squinted at Molly. "No. Molly knows that Donna isn't going to hire us. Right, Moll?"

Molly tried to hold back the tears about to spill over to her cheeks. She slowly shook her head. "She isn't going to call you guys. Well, actually she probably already did leave a message for you to tell you that she isn't going to hire you."

"Why, though? Did she say why?" Sara looked like a little girl who'd just been told she

41

wouldn't be going to the zoo.

"She didn't exactly say why, just that she hired me and Amber for evenings and weekends. I start on Monday." Molly bit her fingernail. "Are you guys mad?"

"Mad? Of course not," Jess said matter-of-factly. "In fact, I figured this is how it would go. Congratulations."

Molly shielded her eyes from the sun and peered at Jess closely, waiting for a glimmer of jealousy. She seemed to mean what she said, but how could Molly be sure?

"Yeah, congrats." Sara smiled, but the corners of her mouth quivered. She looked away, the disappointment evident in her dark eyes.

Molly slapped her jeans and got to her feet. "Look, I don't have to take the job. It wasn't my idea anyway, and it was something we wanted to do together. Why don't I just turn it down?"

Sara's eyes lit up for a second before they darkened again. "No. That wouldn't make any sense."

Jess shook her head right away. "No way! You're taking the job. After all, we only really need one of us to get the discount. Sara and I will just have to figure out other ways to make money so we can use it."

Molly laughed and exhaled deeply. "You're always thinking, Jess. But I'm sure there are rules about the discount. We'll have to wait and see."

She checked herself in the mirror at least a dozen times before she left her room. Then, passing the hall mirror on the way to the front door, she smoothed her hair and straightened her sweater one more time. She patted to make sure the back pockets of her jeans were buttoned down and decided that she looked as good as she could. . . . *Oops.* She scampered back up the stairs to her room. Accessories. A few minutes later, with a necklace hanging from her neck and matching earrings dangling from her ears, she finally felt ready to go.

Molly checked her watch at least a dozen times while she perused the racks of jeans at Magna. Twenty minutes to go. She decided to use the time to memorize the styles and cuts of the jeans.

I'll never figure it all out.

Donna stepped out of the back room and brightened when she saw Molly. "Hi there. Doing some shopping?"

"Oh, I'm just nervous I won't remember all of the stuff I need to know about the clothes. I'm just trying to get a head start."

"Good for you. You don't have to worry about that, though. I'm quite sure you'll catch on. There were lots of reasons I hired you, but the main reason was the look I saw in your eyes. I think you have an instinct for this. You're going to surprise yourself with how much you love it. Every once in a while I find someone who just gets it. I think that you're one of those people."

"Wow. Thanks, D–"

"Amber just got here. Let's go catch up with her and get started."

At Donna's lead, the girls followed her into the back room.

"Welcome to the Magna team, girls!" Donna sorted through a pile of papers she held and nodded her head toward the training table. Molly sat in the same chair she had used in the interview. Still scary, but in a different way.

Donna explained how to fill out the paperwork and told them to watch the two videos when they were finished. "We're also going to do some fun things like role-playing and maybe a game or two before we're done at nine o'clock tonight. Then, for your next training session, you'll be shadowing another sales associate on the sales floor." Her heels clicked on the concrete as she hurried out to help customers.

Molly put her pen down and cracked her knuckles. Amber finished just after Molly and stacked their papers together while Molly picked up the remote control to start the first video. It talked about the company, various media success stories, and had a segment celebrating Magna's rapid growth. The second one focused on theft or, as they called it, loss prevention. *Finally, something interesting. More money is lost to retail companies each year through employee theft than anything else? Shocking!*

Donna poked her head in just as the credits rolled. She clapped her hands together energetically and said, "Okay. I'm sure you're tired of sitting back here in this cold, dark storeroom. How about if we shake things up a bit?" She sat one hip on the edge of the table.

"I'm a customer. I just rushed in and said to you, the first sales person I saw, 'Help! I have a party to go to in three hours, and I have nothing to wear. I gained ten pounds, and nothing fits! I need something cute—fast!' Now, you both go out into the store and pick out the outfit that you would recommend to her. Anything goes. Use your creativity. You have fifteen minutes, go!" Donna glanced at her watch.

Molly and Amber scurried out to the sales floor and scattered in two different directions. Amber went toward the plus-size clothing, presumably because of the customer's weight gain. Molly went right for the jeans. Holding up the jeans to her own frame, she sensed that her customer had just gained enough to make her uncomfortable in her current wardrobe but hadn't quite crossed into the plus-size department.

Every outfit starts with a great pair of jeans. She held up several styles and read their descriptions. Molly settled on one that she thought would be more flattering to a curvier girl: It sat a bit higher on the waist and slightly fuller through the hips.

Jeans draped over one arm, she headed for the tops. There. A long-sleeved white T-shirt and a short-sleeved, black flyaway cardigan that would be flattering on any body shape. Having used only a few of her fifteen minutes, Molly went to the accessories tower and selected some red items to round out the look. She picked out some chunky jewelry and cute red and black high-heeled shoes.

Armed with her selections, she returned to the back room. *Ooh!* She had an idea. With six minutes remaining, Molly decided to put her outfit on one of the lonely, naked mannequins hiding in the corner. She tried to pull the clothes on over the mannequin's arms, but they just wouldn't stretch. Trying to free the sleeve, she knocked the arm and it came loose. She stared at the amputated arm in her hand. *Uh-oh! But wait. . . .* Molly looked closer and realized that it was meant to come off. She easily took both arms off and slipped the tops on.

Squeak. The back room door opened, and then Molly heard the *click-clack* of Donna's high heels. It sounded like she was putting some boxes away in the shoe room which shared the wall Molly stood behind. She hurriedly finished accessorizing her mannequin with the jewelry she'd selected, hoping Donna wouldn't look until she finished. Molly hauled her mannequin to the other side of the room and pushed it behind a screen. She sat down at the training area with only seconds to spare.

Amber made it back to the training area just

before she ran out of time. She stopped short when she saw Molly. "Oh. . .I. . .we. . . I was done a long time ago. I was just shopping."

"Great! Everyone's on time," Donna said from her office in her cheerful, upbeat way. She came out and took a seat at the table with them. "Let's see what you've found for our troubled customer. Amber, why don't you start?"

"I wasn't sure of her size, but since weight gain had been mentioned, I went to the plus-size section and picked out these jeans and this sweater. I think both look stylish but offer her the comfort she needs and coverage for any troublesome spots." Amber blushed and quickly sat in her chair.

"Great, Amber. I really like how you thought of your customer's comfort as well as the fact that she'd want to camouflage any trouble areas. Good job. How about you, Molly?"

Molly stood up and moved her mannequin out to the center. Donna looked impressed, and Amber's jaw dropped. Pretending not to notice their surprise, Molly started right in. "Well, this is what I selected. I just put it all on this mannequin because I had a few extra minutes and I thought it would be easier to see. First, I picked this cut of jeans because of the higher waist and roomier hips." She placed both hands on the mannequin's hips and then around her waist. "I went with a wider belt to give her waist more definition. I chose this flyaway cardigan because it skims the midsection without hugging in any of those unflattering places and nips in here, giving her shape." Molly gestured to the rib cage area and then continued.

"I went with a long-sleeved white tee for underneath. I chose this chunky red jewelry to bring some color into the outfit." She lifted the necklace. "Again, not knowing her exact size, I chose a long necklace because sometimes a chunkier, tighter choker can shorten the neck, but these long lines will make her seem taller."

Donna looked startled.

Knowing she had made an impact, Molly tried to hide her growing excitement. "I gave her a fun coordinating bag to carry and these killer high heels, which I'm going to have to buy for myself. Our customer is all ready for her party."

Donna stared openmouthed. "Molly, if I didn't know better, I'd think that you were a highly trained retail professional. You explained your choices like a seasoned trainer, definitely not like a trainee." Donna shook her head as she looked back to the mannequin.

Molly mumbled her thanks and looked down, embarrassed. *Did I go too far?*

Stepping back into the moment, Donna said, "Well, I don't have much to add, girls. You both made wise choices and had good reasons for what you picked. You also listened to your customer and focused on what she needed, not just on what you like. That's great." She paused for a moment before continuing, choosing her next words carefully.

"Again, though, Molly, you were focused on creating a whole look, not just on selling an item or two. Your customer would have left happy with either of these outfits. But she would have left feeling like a million bucks with Molly's. Can you see the difference?" She waited for them to nod in agreement. "Okay, great job, girls. That wraps up our training session for the evening. You can clock out like I showed you and take off for the evening."

"Thanks so much, Donna." Molly stood to leave but looked at the mannequin. Should she put the clothes away? *Well, if I don't do it, Donna will have to—probably shouldn't cause my new boss extra work.* Molly unbuttoned the top button of the sweater.

Halfway to the back room door, Amber

stopped in her tracks and looked back at Molly. She sighed heavily and then came back to get her clothes to put away. "I can see you're going to make this job a lot more work for me than it has to be—just to keep up with you."

Mmm. Hot chocolate. The smell greeted Molly as soon as she walked into the house. It hadn't even turned cold enough for a jacket yet, but anytime was a good time for her mom's special brew made with homemade fudge sauce and real cream. Molly selected one of the two steaming mugs waiting at the kitchen table and blew on the frothy foam.

"I want to hear all about your first day at work." Molly's mom picked up the other mug.

Settling into her familiar seat at the kitchen dinette, Molly let the steam envelop her face before taking a sip. *Hmm.* Where to start? She told her mom all about her night and everything that Donna had said to her from their first encounter before the training began to the story of the last training session with the mannequin. "Mom, I really wasn't trying to show Amber up. I just did what I thought would make Donna happy and what seemed logical to me. I'm afraid I really made Amber mad, though. Do you think I went too far?"

Molly heard her dad's favorite chair squeak in the living room around the corner. Until then she hadn't realized that he'd been listening from the other room. "Sweetie, as someone who has had employees for years and years, let me give you a piece of insight." He walked into the kitchen and took a sip of hot cocoa from his wife's cup.

Molly looked up at her dad with rapt attention. If anyone knew about the subject of business, he did.

"Workers come and go. Employees are a dime a dozen. But associates, true business partners, are like gold. You were a partner in that business tonight. It sounds to me like the other girl is an employee like most good workers are. She'll probably do fine, but she'll never love it like it seems you do. Donna knows the difference." He squinted and rubbed his chin. "You know, though, it takes all kinds of people to have a successful business. Just like worker bees are necessary to the hive. But one thing you never want to do is hide your work ethic or passion, Moll, just to make a worker bee feel better about her job. Business is business."

Molly nodded. "You're right. I'm there to do a job and to do it well. It would be foolish to skip a good idea or act dumb just to fit in with the others. That's what you're saying, right?"

"That's exactly what I mean."

Mom jumped in. "But, Molly dear, maybe you can find other ways to make Amber and the rest of the girls feel special in their jobs, too. I mean, you don't want to climb to the top on the backs of other people. Just acknowledge their efforts now and then. If you have a question that they might know the answer to, humble yourself and ask them—give them a chance."

Dad nodded in agreement and squeezed his wife's shoulder.

"More great advice. What would I do without you guys?" Molly's chair skipped along the tile as she pushed it with the back of her legs and hugged them both. "Now, I have homework to do. I need to learn how to invest all of my vast riches so I can be a retail mogul one day."

Dad shook his head and chuckled as Molly turned to leave.

She barely got through the door before

she stopped in her tracks, darted back into the kitchen, grabbed her mug of hot chocolate, and then hurried up the stairs to her room.

I'm a lucky girl. . . . No, not lucky—blessed.

Chapter 4

TRUCE AND VICTORY

Molly groaned and covered her head with her comforter. Was she dreaming?

"Molly, you have a phone call!"

Ugh. Eight o'clock on Saturday morning? Who could be calling? What a long week—midterms, homework, extra shifts for training. . . .

"Molly!" Her mom grew more insistent.

"I'm coming. I'm coming," Molly mumbled as she swung her legs over the side of the bed and padded down the stairs, rubbing her eyes.

"It's Donna," Mrs. Jacobs whispered, covering the receiver with her hand.

Molly cleared her throat and hoped she'd sound awake. "Hello, this is Molly."

"Molly? Oh, thank God!" Donna sounded

frantic. "I'm sorry to bother you on your day off. But Heather, one of the girls you haven't met, just quit on me. She was supposed to work from ten to three today, and she just called to say that she isn't coming back. I'm really in a bind. I know that you've had a long week, but is there any way you could pick up Heather's shift today?"

Molly chewed her bottom lip. "Um. . .can you hold on for a second while I talk to my mom? In fact, how about if I give you a call back in just a few minutes. I need to work a few things out. Just a few minutes, okay?"

"Perfect! Thanks so much, Molly. I'll be waiting to hear from you—I'll need to know as soon as possible, though."

Molly plopped down on the couch and grabbed an afghan to pull over her body for just one more minute. Did she even want to work? But Donna would be mad if she said no. *Okay, I'm already up, have no homework, Donna's in a bind—but there's the swim party tonight. That's okay—I'll do both. Now to clear it with Mom.*

"Molls, I just don't want this to be a regular occurrence. Okay? Go ahead and do it because it doesn't interfere with anything else, and I'm available to give you a ride. But if you

had homework or your youth group party was
during the day, I'd say no. Understood?"

"Yep. I get it, Mom. I'm going to call Donna
back, and then I've got to get ready."

Ahh. The shower perked her up. It would be
her first real sales shift. Now she wouldn't have
to hold herself back from helping customers like
she had to do when she shadowed Amy. Molly
dressed in a hurry. *This is going to be so cool!*

Right before she left, she e-mailed Sara
and Jess—no way would she call them before
ten o'clock on a Saturday morning—to let
them know that they were still on for the pool
party they planned to attend that afternoon.
Molly wished they'd come with her to church
sometimes. But at least they were going to
the party, and they came to other fun things
sometimes. They'd come around in time—
Molly was sure of it.

"Thanks so much for helping me out today,
Molly," Donna gushed as soon as she saw
Molly walk into the store. "You obviously aren't
trained to ring up customers, so it will be Amy
and me behind the registers for the next couple
of hours. That means you and Amber are out

on the sales floor alone until Edie gets here at noon. Do you think you can handle it?" She flitted around trying to get the store opened.

"Everything will be fine." Molly clocked in. "I'm looking forward to getting out there with the customers." She rubbed her hands together. "Let me at 'em."

Donna laughed and opened the heavy gate. "Well, I'm here for anything you need. Please don't hesitate to ask me any—"

Molly cut Donna off midsentence when a customer walked in under the rising gate.

"Hi. Welcome to Magna. What are you shopping for today?" Molly got off to the right start. From the corner of her eye she saw Donna exhale deeply and relax her neck by rotating her head. She must have been worried.

Amber busied herself keeping the racks straightened, putting clothes away when customers left them in the fitting rooms, and helping customers when they sought her attention.

Donna took a break from ringing customers. "So Molly, what do you have going on right now?"

Molly looked around the store and pointed to the fitting rooms. "I have a mom and daughter in the first dressing room. The daughter wants to try on the white sweater on the mannequin in the window. So I'm about to go get that for her." She looked toward the front. "Let's see. That family over there is shopping for a gift for their cousin's birthday. See the two girls in back? The tall one is a bride-to-be, and she's looking for honeymoon clothes. I have fitting rooms started for all of them. . .gotta go." She walked away before Donna could ask anything else. *I hope that wasn't rude. Customers first.*

Molly pulled the mannequin out of the window display and took the sweater off. As she backed up, she almost tripped over a girl digging through a stack of T-shirts with her three friends standing beside her. "Oops! Sorry!" Molly's jaw dropped when she realized who it was. She stood face-to-face with the three most popular girls in her grade and one very popular junior.

"I. . .um. . .I. . . Can I. . . ," she stammered and stuttered. *Get it together, Molly.* She had a job to do. "I have a customer in the fitting room who's waiting for this." She held up the white sweater that she had retrieved from the window display. "I'll take it to her and then be right back to help you find what you need. Okay?"

"Great! Thanks, Molly." Kim, the junior, spoke for all of them.

Molly stepped away for just a moment, but the four girls left before she got back. *Phew.* Time passed quickly and three o'clock came much faster than she expected.

Donna peered over her shoulder at the clock-in screen and said, "Your break's not listed. You must have forgotten to sign out for it. I'll take care of that for you. What time did you. . . Wait a second. Did you even get a break at all today?" Donna looked horrified.

"Oh, it's no big deal." Molly waved her hand. "I was enjoying myself and didn't even notice. I know it's my responsibility to make sure I get one. I'll remember next time."

"Okay. Let's not make it a habit, though. I can't have you burning out on me." Donna walked Molly toward the front of the store. "You were amazing today. I think you're the best hiring decision I've ever made. You really seem to enjoy yourself with the customers, and you stay so organized, even in the face of pressure. Just keep up the good work!" She started to walk away but had one more thing to add. "But don't be a hero, okay? Speak up."

Molly grinned. "Thank you so much, Donna. I promise to take care of myself."

"All right. Now get on out of here. I heard you have a pool party to go to!"

"Cannonbaaaall!" *SPLASH!*

"Oh no! It's one of those kinds of parties, huh?" Jess laughed as they climbed out of the car with their beach towels and bags.

"I guess so. But that's okay. It'll be worth it when you taste Pastor Mike's burgers," Molly promised and pushed the car door closed. "He does something amazing with them. He adds oatmeal and eggs, I think. Oh, and lots of garlic salt. I'm already starving, just thinking about them!"

"I'm just thirsty right now. Do you think they have diet soda?" Sara wondered.

Thwack! SPLASH!

"What on earth are they doing back there?" Molly laughed as they went through the gate into the backyard. One of the church members had offered the youth group the use of their heated pool one last time before the Wisconsin autumn set in. "I sure hope the owners are out of town." They went around the corner through the walkway of shrubs and turned to look at the pool.

Thwack! SPLASH!

Molly's head snapped back as a wall of water slammed into her. All the boys, the dry girls on the other side of the pool, and Jess and Sara just laughed. Molly gritted her teeth and felt like she could hit someone.

"This is a new outfit, and I fixed my hair. I wasn't even planning to get it wet, but now everything's drenched." Why was she whining? She begged herself to stop but just couldn't.

"Oh, it'll be okay. You look just fine," Jess said, wringing out her towel.

"It is a pool party after all, Molls—everyone's wet. Come on, smile." Sara grinned. She lowered her voice to a whisper, still smiling. "You don't want people to think you're a poor sport."

Molly took a deep breath and blew the air slowly from her lungs. "You're right. I'll lighten up." She stripped off her soaked cover-up, revealing her new one-piece suit, and then gestured to Jess and Sara. "Hey, cute suits, you guys."

"Thanks. Mine's new. I can't ever wear a

one-piece." Jess tugged on the waistband of the bottoms of her red-and-white-striped two-piece. "They don't make them long enough."

Sara wore a purple tankini with swim shorts. "You know why I wear these." She patted her hips.

Molly and Jess looked at each other and rolled their eyes. Changing the subject, Molly said, "Okay. Come on, girls. Since we're already wet, let's show these boys what a real cannonball is." She winked and tied her hair back in a ponytail.

"You don't mean. . . ?" Jess looked horrified.

"Oh, yes I do. Come on!"

Making eye contact with no one, the three girls walked expressionless to the diving board. All eyes were on them—something was up. They looked at each other—still no expression—and stepped up onto the board. Sara went first. She took off in a run and jumped as hard as she could.

Thwack! Immediately she tucked into a cannonball pose and landed with all her might on the surface of the water. *Splash!*

The instant Sara's feet lifted from the board, Jess had taken off running across it. She took advantage of the spring in the board from the momentum of Sara's jump. It flung her even higher and harder than Sara, and she caused an even bigger splash.

Thwack! SPLASH!

Molly did the exact same thing immediately following Jess's jump.

THWACK! SPLASH!!!

When all three of them surfaced, the whole group erupted into cheers. "You win, you win! We give—truce?" A drenched Pastor Mike shouted from his perch on a deck chair.

When the roar settled into a soft buzz, he called out, "I think it's time for some burgers; what do you think?"

Thirty minutes later they were all seated around the pool deck. Some were on deck chairs, some sat right on the concrete. A few of them were a little ways off in the grass. Everyone had a plate with a thick burger and a big helping of Mrs. Beck's mustard potato salad.

With the students' mouths too full of food to talk, Pastor Mike took the opportunity. "Hey, gang, did you see what happened when Sara, Jess, and Molly jumped into the pool like they did?"

"You call that jumping?" one of the boys called out from the back. Everyone laughed.

"Good point. But whatever you want to call

it, did you see what happened when they did it? First Sara went. Her cannonball caused a pretty reasonable splash, but when Jess followed right in her footsteps, the splash, the water displacement, and the level of bystander soakage was much, much higher."

"Tell me about it!" Brad Beck rolled his eyes and laughed.

"Molly went next. The momentum of her jump was fueled by the two who went before her. She couldn't have pulled back the power of that jump even if she wanted to. If she had decided at the last moment that she didn't want to do it, she wouldn't have been able to do a thing about it. She was committed to her choice whether she liked it or not."

Molly glanced around her. All eyes were on Pastor Mike.

"A lot of life is very much like that. When one person leads the way and others follow directly in the path of those footsteps, misdeeds or wrongdoings become easier and easier while the effects of them grow deeper and much further reaching, causing much more damage every step of the way. By the time it was Molly's turn to jump, she got the credit—or, depending on how you look at it, the blame—for the biggest splash."

"We'll go with blame." Brad jumped in again.

"I just want to challenge you all not to let yourselves get pulled along in the wake of other kids' splashes this school year. Be aware of the momentum of other people's actions so that you don't just get pulled along in their wake to go further and faster than you'd intended."

Molly looked around the group—some of them were still paying attention to their pastor; others had become completely disinterested, like Jess. She turned off her attention when anything reminded her of church. *I've got to pray for her. Sara, too, of course, but Jess most of all.*

Molly snapped her attention back to the pastor. ". . .have any prayer requests or concerns? If not, we'll close in prayer, and you can get back to your swimming."

"I have something to say, Pastor Mike, if that's okay." Brad stood up.

"Sure, Brad." Pastor Mike seemed eager—probably glad to have someone participate in the discussion.

"I just want to offer a cannonball truce and name the girls the winners."

Pastor Mike rolled his eyes and threw his hands up in the air, laughing.

Brad picked up his white towel and waved it in the air. "I think we ought to give it a rest, or there won't be any water left in the pool. What do you say, Moll?" Everyone laughed and waited for Molly's response.

Molly stood and took a bow. "We accept the truce and the victory."

Chapter 5

WHAT ARE "FRIENDS" FOR?

Molly felt someone behind her as she put her books in her locker the first thing Monday morning. Her books slipped from the stack at the bottom of her locker to the tile floor. She struggled to set order to her things before they were spread across the hallway. Finally she could turn around. Expecting to see Sara and Jess, Molly jumped when she saw Kim—the popular junior who had been in the store on Saturday—and her three friends, Pam, Marcy, and Jade. Surprised, Molly waited for someone to speak.

Kim put her arm across Molly's shoulders. "So, Molly, how are you today?"

"I'm great, Kim. What's up? I only have a minute or two before class." *Since when do they like me? I'd better watch out for these girls—they're up to no good.*

"Sure—us, too. We just wanted to talk to you about something." She looked down at the pointy red toe of her shoe—the same red shoes Molly had used to outfit her mannequin on her first day of training.

Molly's radar turned to high alert. Something just didn't seem right. "Okay. . . ? What's up?"

"Well, you have the coolest job at the best store. And I was thinking—well, I should say, we were thinking—that you might like to share your discount with us now and then. You see, we both have something that the other wants, and we can help each other get it."

Ah. So that's it. "Um. . .what exactly do you have that I want?" *The nerve.*

Kim steered Molly down the hall with her arm still draped over her shoulder. "Well, let's face it. In this school, I have—*we* have—the power to make or break someone's reputation. With us on your side, you could be one of the most popular girls. But with us against you, high school as you know it would be over."

Molly stared at Kim with her mouth open. What nerve to come right out and say that!

They never had anything to do with her before this. *Ugh.* If she didn't do it, things could get really bad, but if she did, she'd be one of the popular girls. *But at what price?*

"I don't know, Kim. I mean, I could get into lots of trouble for that. I could lose my job."

"Oh Molly, you'll never get caught. We'll just try it once or twice. Okay?"

"You're going to have to let me think about it." Molly hesitated. *I've got to get out of here.* "I've got to go now. Talk to you later."

Later that afternoon, at the lunch table with Sara and Jess, Molly just picked at her food. "What's wrong, Molly?" Sara furrowed her eyebrows.

"Hmm?" She looked up, elbow on the table, her head in her hands. "Oh, nothing," she replied and then shook her head. "That's not really true. Something is wrong. People are trying to get me to use my discount on clothes for them."

"Who?" Jess demanded. She sat up straighter and looked around.

"Oh, that doesn't matter. The point is that I don't want to be in that position, and I don't know what to do about it."

At that moment, Kim and company walked by, squeezing between students seated on the lunch table benches. As she sidled by Molly, Kim reached down and squeezed Molly's shoulder and gave her a quick wink.

"Never mind. I know who it is." Jess rolled her eyes in disgust. "It figures."

"So, what are you going to do about it?" Sara asked. "I mean, can you even do that?"

"It's really against the rules. I could lose my job. Not to mention, it's dishonest." Molly took a small bite.

"But I thought we were going to. . ." Jess looked confused.

"I know, Jess." Molly waved her hand. "Don't worry about it. I figured out a way to share with you guys that wouldn't actually be wrong."

Sara's eyes lit up, and she sat forward. "Really? How?"

Molly pulled apart her sandwich and scowled at it. She dropped it back onto her lunch tray. "The discount is given as a perk for employees but also to make sure that we can wear the clothes for work. So, I figure that as long as you guys use the discount on stuff I can also borrow and wear to work once in a while, it would be okay."

"Great idea. It's a win-win." Jess looked impressed.

"It's better than nothing. But that means no jeans for me." Sara put her uneaten cookie back in her bag.

"Maybe I could buy you a pair of jeans as a birthday gift or something, Sara. We're allowed to do that." Molly laughed. "It'll be okay. You can eat your cookie." She winked at Jess and then looked back at Sara. "Skipping one cookie isn't going to change your whole body type anyway."

"And Sara, for the last time. . . You're. Not. Fat." Jess softly pounded her fists on the table with each syllable.

"Oh, I know. I know. I'm just shaped differently." Sara rolled her eyes.

"What I wouldn't give for your waist—instead of looking like a little boy." Molly sighed and drank the last of her juice.

"So, back to the situation with Kim. What are you going to do?" Jess wadded up her trash and lobbed it into a nearby trash can.

"Well, I'm not going to share my discount." Molly looked up at the ceiling. "I wish there was a middle ground. A way to keep them happy but not break any rules." There had to be a way.

"I've got it!"

Sara jumped, startled at Molly's outburst. "Got what?"

"I know just what to do to keep everyone happy but not get into any trouble." Molly waited for Sara and Jess to become interested.

"Well? Let's have it," Jess demanded.

"We have these things called Bounty Bucks. During the next ten days we're giving a ten-dollar Bounty Buck to customers for every fifty dollars they spend."

"Oh yeah, I've used those," Sara chimed in. "My sister and I saved them up. You get them at one visit, and then you go back at a later time to use them as free money."

"Exactly. Like a coupon," Molly explained. "What if I give Jess and her friends a bunch of those to use? It wouldn't be sharing my discount, and they're only coupons. It's not like it's free merchandise. I wonder if that would make them happy."

"Can you do that?" Jess sounded excited.

"I don't see why not. I'll just have to grab a handful of 'bucks.' They're out at the cash register for us to give out to customers."

"Perfect!" Jess and Sara agreed.

They all stepped over the bench to leave the lunchroom.

"So, when can we go shopping?" Jess asked.

"We'll have to do it like we're just out

shopping—you know, trying on clothes but not buying. Then I'll have to go back and use my discount to buy the clothes you picked out. And remember, they have to be things I can wear, and I'll have to wear them to work at least once. Okay?"

"Okay. Sounds good." Sara nodded.

"So, when?" Jess asked again.

"Well, I work tonight and tomorrow. Youth group is on Wednesday, so how about Thursday after school?"

"Great. We can hang out at the mall for a while. I've been saving my allowance, and my grandma already sent my birthday money." Sara stopped at the door to her classroom, waved, and went in.

"Sounds great." Jess went into the room across the hall.

Molly continued down the hall alone toward her biology class.

Waiting just to the right of the door to Molly's class, leaning back with one foot up against the wall, stood Kim. She looked Molly up and down, lingering over Molly's new Magna outfit—jeans, high heels, and a khaki jacket. "Well, what's the verdict? You've had time to think about it. What's it going to be?"

"Kim, I feel like you're pushing me. Would you risk your job if you were me?"

Kim scowled and stared her down.

Whoops. Better talk fast. "But, actually, I have a better idea than sharing my discount. That was expressly forbidden in training. There's no way I can pretend that I didn't know. So, what about this. . ." Molly told Kim all about the Bounty Bucks plan.

At first Kim stared skeptically. "I don't see how. . ."

"Just let me finish explaining."

By the time Molly finished explaining, Kim looked like she understood. "So the ten-dollar Bounty Bucks are really just like gift certificates." She looked puzzled. "Hmm. That's way better than sharing the discount. How can you get away with that?"

"I don't think it's as bad as sharing my discount, because it was never mentioned as not being allowed," Molly explained. "The coupons are there for us to pass out. How would it be wrong?"

Kim snorted, shaking her head. "Okay, it's your call. So, you're going to get me some of those Bounty Buck things then?"

"Yeah. I work tonight, so unless something

has changed at work I'll be able to get them tonight, and I'll give them to you tomorrow. But Kim, you have to promise that this is it. You won't bug me for other stuff from my work."

"Yeah, sure, whatever." Kim laughed as she sauntered away.

"Molly, I've got you on fitting rooms and cash register tonight. I really prefer to have you on the sales floor, because it's where you do best. But I do need you to learn how to work the cash wrap." Donna spoke fast. "Since it's supposed to be pretty slow tonight, I figured it would be a good time. Amy will be close by if you need her. I'm leaving for the day. So, any questions before I head out of here?" Donna, already buttoning her jacket, was clearly in a hurry.

"Nope, no questions. I'm good. Have a great night."

Amy looked annoyed as she approached with the clipboard in her hand. "Hey, Molly. How's it going? Okay, your sales goal is only five hundred dollars, because you'll be on register. You have a goal of two credit card sign-ups. Oh, and don't forget to hand out the Bounty Bucks to everyone who comes through the line. They get one for every fifty dollars they spend. Any questions?"

Molly shook her head quizzically at Amy's curt demeanor.

"Good. I'm going to take my dinner break. Amber will be here in about twenty minutes." She rolled her eyes. "So just hold down the fort while I'm gone. I'll just be in the back room. Come get me if someone needs to be rung up."

Molly looked around the empty store. *No one in sight—perfect.* She walked over to the cash register and grabbed the next week's schedule, pretending to look at it. She wasn't doing anything wrong. Was she? *If it's not wrong, why am I so nervous—and why do I have to hide it?* "It's just like coupons in the paper," she whispered. *Then why does it feel different?*

She put the schedule back and busied herself straightening the bags. Molly looked around the store one more time and then grabbed a thick stack of the coupons and put them in the cargo pocket of her khaki pants. *Snap.* She secured the pocket, just in case. She took a deep breath and exhaled, trying to settle her stomach. She would give the coupons to Kim and then never do anything like this again. It wasn't over yet, though. For the rest of her shift Molly

battled her inner voice. *Don't do it. Don't do it.*
Too late.

"Here." Molly slapped the Bounty Bucks on the
table in front of Kim where she sat at the lunch
table with Pam, Marcy, and Jade. "There are
five of them here for each of you. I don't ever
want to hear of this again, though. Promise me
you won't hold this over my head or ask me for
more. I can't get more. Besides, the promotion
ends in a few days, and that will be it anyway.
Okay?" The four girls looked at Molly in
surprise.

Molly wasn't sure if they were surprised that
she actually got the coupons or if they were
surprised by her tone. She hoped it was both—
and that they took her seriously. *This could get
bad if they don't.*

"So, what exactly do we do with these?" Kim
turned them over to read the instructions.

"You just take them to the store on one
of these days," Molly explained, pointing to
the dates printed on the coupon. "You can use
them just like cash. They are redeemable for
merchandise, even if you don't buy anything at
all." *Oops.* The light dawned as Molly realized

exactly how these were different than coupons. "But think about it. If you walk in there with five of these, since they are only given with a fifty-dollar purchase, that's like saying you had spent two hundred fifty dollars to earn the coupons. There's no way you guys spent that much. The manager would remember if you had. So, when you use them, just use one or two at a time and buy something else to go with it. Okay?" *What have I done?*

"Okay. That makes sense," Kim said, and the other girls nodded.

Kim motioned with her head for the other three to leave with her. She patted Molly on the shoulder. "Hey, thanks, Molly. You're a cool kid."

Chapter 6

HANGING IN
THE BALANCE

"This is only your third week of work, and you're already asking if you can skip church tonight?" Dad didn't like it at all. "This is where the rubber meets the road, Molly. It's time to put your money where your mouth is."

Molly rolled her eyes at her dad's incessant use of clichés. Usually she found it charming—cute, even. But when she was being lectured, she couldn't stand it.

"Hey, I don't appreciate you rolling your eyes at me. You're the one who promised to hold up your end of the bargain. But now you're testing the waters to see what you can get away with. Sorry, Moll. I'm going to hold you to your word.

You're going to have to find out if it's even possible for you to handle so many irons in the fire."

She couldn't take even one more trite saying. "Okay, Dad. You're right. I'll be fine. I just thought it might be easier to have a catch-up night than to have to stay up late."

"I'll tell you when you can catch up—after school tomorrow instead of going shopping with the girls." Molly's mom teased her, knowing that the last thing she'd want to give up would be a trip to the mall with her friends. "No? Okay, well then I guess it's not all bad. Now, go get your things. It's time to leave for church."

After the short drive, Molly entered the gymnasium at church and immediately heard someone call her name. She looked across the crowded dodgeball game to locate the source of the voice. *Sara!* She had come without any prodding from Molly. *Weird.* Just as she pondered Sara's reasons for coming, *SMACK!* The ball slapped across the side of Molly's face. Her head snapped back, and her cheek flamed where the ball had struck.

For a second she was stunned and felt nothing. Then the sting set in, and it felt like a mild burn. Like a bee sting it continued to get worse until it felt like it was on fire. *Don't cry!* Trying not to look angry or start crying from the shock and the embarrassment—not to mention the pain—she hurried across the gym, past the openmouthed onlookers, to the kitchen. Sara followed her.

Sue, one of the youth leaders, jogged into the kitchen behind them. "You okay, hon?"

Molly nodded. Afraid she was going to lose her grip on her composure, she didn't trust herself to speak just yet.

In silence, Sue put together a makeshift ice pack. Molly hopped up onto the kitchen counter and held the ice on her cheek and sipped a soda that Sara had poured for her.

After a few minutes, Molly gained more control of her emotions. Sue looked right into her eyes and asked, "So, you okay?"

"Oh yeah, I'm fine. It's just that things are so physical all the time. I want to be a girl, and these boys are always splashing, throwing, shoving, pushing. . . . It just gets tiring. I want to be treated like a lady, you know? And then when something like this happens, I have a hard time not getting really angry, and I wind up looking like a blubbering idiot. It's just not fair."

"No, it's not fair, Molly. Sorry to say, it's part of life though. Boys are more physical, and they play that way—sometimes their whole lives." Sue laughed and shook her head. "Girls who are becoming women want different things. And, sometimes, that transition from being a girl to being a woman doesn't have a clear line dividing it, and the boys get mixed signals." She cocked her head and gave Molly a pointed look. "Like when you guys cannonballed the other day. From where I sat, it looked like you got pretty physical." She peered intently at both of them.

"Yeah, but only because we were slammed in the face with water the minute we got there. And that was another time I nearly lost my temper."

"Moll, you're changing. Your hormones are changing. It's going to take you some time to learn how to deal with the different thoughts and emotions you're having. The best advice I can give you is to just be honest." Sue hopped up to sit on the counter beside her. "When something happens, like when you got slammed in the face with water, instead of jumping in and fighting back, say something like, 'I really wish you'd treat me with respect, like a lady.'"

She lifted the ice pack to peek at Molly's

cheek and pressed it back down. "You have to let them know what you want and not send mixed signals and then wonder why they haven't caught on. Do you know what I'm saying?"

Molly repositioned her ice pack. "I do. I hadn't thought of it that way before, though. I don't mean to send mixed signals—that's for sure. I'm going to have to try to remember that."

"You know, what you said really makes sense," Sara chimed in. "I guess we're the ones changing—not them, really. How are they to know things are different?"

"Honesty. Hmm. Worth a try." Molly smiled and jumped off the counter. "My face feels better now. Maybe we could go join the group?"

"Take out a No. 2 pencil, and put all of your books and belongings under your desk. You'll have fifty minutes to complete this test. . . ," Molly's biology teacher's voice droned.

Molly stared with her mouth wide open, horrified that she'd forgotten about the test. Would it have mattered if she had remembered? When could she have studied? Molly surveyed the classroom. All the other students sat with their pencils poised, ready to begin the test.

She fumbled in her bag to get what she needed. Saying a little prayer, she started to read.

Uh-oh. By the third question, Molly knew she was in trouble. She'd never be able to just wing this test. It was all new information she could only have learned by studying—but she hadn't.

Even if she bombed the test, she could eventually bring her grade up, and she planned to talk to Donna about scheduling her either Monday or Tuesday, instead of both nights in a row. But, in the meantime, her parents would see this grade, and she'd been warned that if her grades slipped, her job would have to go. So Molly knew she'd better do some of her best guessing. She grimaced at the paper in her hands. *How do you guess when you don't even know what the words mean?*

Sure that she'd bombed her test, Molly slumped into the hallway. How had she let that happen? She dragged her way through the school and out the front door toward the waiting bus where Sara and Jess were probably already saving her a seat. At that thought she immediately brightened. *Time to go shopping!* She climbed aboard the bus and saw Jess and Sara in the middle. She maneuvered between the seats to get to the open seat beside Sara.

"Hey, you two! Ready to do some shopping?"

"Oh yeah. I can't wait." Sara grinned and held up the money she'd been counting.

Jess held up a finger as she finished up a call on her cell phone. "Okay, I'll be home by seven. . . . Yes, Sara's mom is picking us up and she'll drop me off. . . . Yes, I'll be careful. Why all the worry all of a sudden? . . . Okay, no big deal. See ya then."

"What was that about?" Molly asked.

"Oh, she goes in phases. You know how moms are. Well, come to think of it, you probably don't know. Your mom is always worried about you."

Molly laughed. "I don't know who's worse, my mom or my dad." She leaned her head back on her seat, sighing deeply. "I really need this diversion. I've had better days. . .but I'm leaving all of that at school. Let's go have some fun."

They were on a different bus than the one they usually rode—one that would drop them near the mall. They walked over to the mall and then called home to let everyone know they'd made it safely. They were even planning on eating dinner together at the mall—a first for them. But first—Magna.

"Molly!" Amy grinned as soon as she saw Molly come into the store.

Molly chuckled and shook her head. She never could figure out Amy's moods.

"Are you working with me tonight? I thought it was Amber on the schedule."

"Nope. Not me. This is just a shopping visit. Amy, I'm not sure if you met my friends when they were in before. This is Sara and Jess."

Both girls had learned from their hesitation last time and immediately reached out to shake Amy's hand and tell her that they were pleased to meet her.

"Hey Amy, is Donna here? I really need to talk to her."

"Yeah, but she's on the phone. I'll let her know you need to see her when she gets off."

The girls started their shopping. As usual they started in the jeans section—they were the most important item, after all. At seventy-five dollars a pair, the choice was tough. But each of them hoped to find the perfect pair that day. Jess was long and very lean, so she had her pick of styles. Sara had slightly curvier hips but a very tiny waist which made things a bit more difficult. Plus, she was the shortest of them. Molly was average in every way—height and weight, right in the middle.

"Don't worry, girls. There's a perfect pair of jeans in these racks for each of us. I promise." Molly grinned and started digging.

They each took six or seven pairs to the fitting rooms and began trying them on. The girls were each trying to pull on a pair when they heard a knock on the door. They stopped giggling and said, "Who is it?" Which, for some reason, made them giggle even more.

"Sounds like you girls are having fun in there." Donna laughed. "It's just me, Donna. Did you want to talk to me, Molly?"

Molly hurried to button the pair of jeans she'd been trying on. "I'll be right out."

She opened the fitting room door just a crack and squeezed through it because Jess hadn't gotten her next pair of jeans on yet. "Hi Donna. Sorry, were we being too loud?"

"Oh, not at all, Molly. You girls have fun. You deserve it. Now, what can I do for you?" She had her purse in her hand and her jacket over her arm. It looked like Molly had caught her on her way out again.

"Oh, well, I won't keep you long. It's just that I wanted to talk to you about the schedule if that's okay."

Donna nodded for Molly to continue.

"Well, the past couple of weeks I've been scheduled both Monday and Tuesday nights, and then I have church on Wednesday nights, which is really important to my family, and then usually I have exams on Thursdays." *Slow down, Molly.* She took a deep breath. "So, I'm having a tough time getting all of my studying done. Would it be possible to be scheduled only one of those nights, either Monday or Tuesday and then another night of the week, say Friday night?"

"You mean you want to work on Friday night instead of Tuesday night?" Donna laughed. "I hardly ever get a request like that. But, yeah, that works for me. I'm sure Amber would appreciate being freed up on Friday nights. So, will a schedule like Monday night, Friday night, and Saturday during the day work for you then?"

"That would be just perfect," Molly said. "Maybe once in a while I could work Thursday night instead of Friday or Saturday—once a month, maybe?"

"That sounds great, Molly. Thanks so much for being honest with me about it. I want to be helpful, but I can't if I don't know what you need." Donna smiled. "Now you get back to your fun. I've got to get to a dinner."

Molly squeezed back into the fitting room where Jess and Sara looked triumphant. They had each found the perfect pair of jeans. Since Molly loved the ones she still had on, they called the jean search successful. *Time for tops.*

Sara and Jess each bought a couple of things full price, and Molly set a stack of clothes aside to buy later. In the meantime they wandered the mall.

Sara looked at her watch. "Hey you guys, I'm starving. Can we go eat?"

"Yeah, now that you mention it, I'm hungry, too." Jess rubbed her flat tummy.

"Sounds good to me." Molly agreed.

In the bustling food court they waited in line and got their food. They walked around for a minute or two trying to find a table. When they finally sat down, Molly saw Brad Beck from youth group. When he looked their way, she waved at him.

He wandered over.

"Hi, Brad." Sara spoke first.

"Hi, Sara. How are all of you tonight?" He looked at each of them.

"Oh, just doing some shopping." Molly wondered if she should invite him to join them, but she didn't want to annoy her friends.

"Care to join us?" Sara offered, scooting over on the bench seat so he could sit down if he wanted to.

"I'd love to." He looked around the food court, up and down the row of fast food offerings. "Let me go grab my dinner, and then I'll be back to join you."

Molly watched Sara watch him leave. The light began to dawn. She looked at Jess, who was also staring at Sara as she watched Brad. Jess and Molly raised their eyebrows and nodded knowingly. By unspoken agreement, they remained silent, waiting to see how long it took Sara to snap out of it. Her big blue eyes were locked on one tall figure all the way across the food court, and they were seeing nothing else.

After a minute or two, Sara jumped out of her daydream. Too late. She had more than given herself away.

"Okay, you've been holding out on us. What gives? What's with you and Brad? You like him, huh?" Molly peppered her.

"I have one question, Sara." Jess had a twinkle in her eye. "And your answer will tell me all I need to know." She paused for impact. "Did you and Brad set up this *chance* meeting ahead of time?"

Oooh. Molly sat forward in her chair. Good question. Not only would the answer tell them whether or not Brad knew that Sara liked him, but it would also tell them if Brad and Sara had spoken outside of church. Molly watched Sara's face as she struggled to think of an answer.

Sara rolled a french fry back and forth in a pile of salted ketchup and shoved it in her mouth. They were still staring at her, so she shrugged and pointed to her mouth and made exaggerated chewing motions.

Brad walked up with a tray of food that would feed an army. Tacos, a few burritos, a big plate of loaded nachos just dripping with cheese, and what looked like a gallon of soda.

The girls eyeballed his food. "Are you going to eat all of that?" Molly sounded horrified.

Brad patted his tummy. "I'm a growing boy."

"I guess!" Jess laughed.

Sara's cheeks were as red as her ketchup-laden french fries that she ate as fast as she could. But the sparkle in her eyes gave her away.

Chapter 7

PROMOTION
COMMOTION

"You've been here just over six weeks, Molly.
I wanted to have a little meeting to talk about
how things are going." Donna held up a finger
and answered her ringing phone.

Molly fidgeted in her seat and picked at a
fingernail. She'd been doing a good job, right?
What if Donna didn't think so? What if she
found out about the Bounty Bucks? Or that she
had shopped for her friends?

"Okay, sorry about that. Where were we?"
Donna hung up the phone and turned back to
Molly.

"Well, let's see." Molly tapped her fingernail
on her glossy lips and pretended to think for a

moment, trying not to smile. "If I remember correctly, you were about to tell me what a fantastic job I've been doing and how you're about to promote me to manager." She kept a straight face and waited.

"Ha, ha. Funny. But, you know, you're not too far from the truth. The thing is, you have been doing a really terrific job, Molly. Did you realize that since your very first sales shift, you have never, ever missed a goal of any kind? Ever." She squinted at Molly and shook her head as though she couldn't imagine such a thing. "That's amazing. You're a very driven employee, and I think you would do well with any job you decided to do. But, in this case, you have one more thing going for you. Passion." She nodded and pressed her fist to her heart. "I think you love what you're doing, and you're a real natural for this type of sales. Can I ask you, Molly, what is it about this job that inspires you?" Donna leaned forward.

"Hmm. I guess I hadn't really thought about it before." She thought for a moment. *Ah.* She had her answer. "You know what it is? It's the rush of knowing that people need my help, and I can help them. It's having a certain knack for a subject that's very important to women." She sat forward in her seat, excited just thinking about it. "And take for example the units-per-sale goal. We're supposed to sell an average of three items to each customer, right?"

Donna nodded, appearing to soak in every word.

"Well, some people think that's just greed on the part of the company, but I get the point. We're not to just sell three things—we're to put together a whole look. It takes at least three items to do that. So, the customer looks better and leaves happier. Magna is more successful, and I'm more successful. But aside from all of that, there's nothing like helping a frantic or depressed customer leave here with a big grin because she feels confident and beautiful."

Donna pondered Molly's words for a moment. "You know what, Molly? Since you've been with us, you've awakened something in me that I've let sleep for a while. I think I've become too business minded and have forgotten about some of those feelings. Since you've been here, I've felt a renewed passion for people, not just my passion for this business. I'm grateful to you for that, and I hope you manage to hang on to it." She looked reflective, so Molly sat quietly until Donna had gathered her thoughts.

"I have an offer for you, Molly." Donna turned all business again. "I want to make you an AMIT, which is an assistant manager in training."

Molly opened her eyes wide. *She's got to be kidding!*

"You can't be an assistant manager until you're seventeen, and even then, I think you'd be the first in the company to be so young. But you can be a key holder at sixteen, which would be the next promotion after this one."

Donna reached down into her file drawer and pulled out some papers. "As an AMIT, you'll train for the assistant manager position so that you're ready when it's time. Over the eighteen months until you're seventeen, you'll learn everything about that job." She pointed to the job description. "You'll learn how to set goals for the sales associates, how to make the schedule, how to process freight, and everything else that goes with being a manager. Your schedule will stay the same, and you'll get a dollar-an-hour raise, plus your discount will go up to 45 percent off full-priced merchandise. What do you think?"

"Really? Wow!" *I can't believe this is happening.* "I just can't believe that you'd take a chance like that with me. Of course I want to do it. I'm so excited!"

"Great. The promotion is effective immediately. Here's your new name tag and your new sign-in password for the computer. Congratulations!" Donna flashed Molly a huge grin and handed her a thick envelope.

"Thank you so much, Donna. You won't be sorry!" Molly hurried from the office so she could put on her new name tag. *Molly Jacobs, AMIT.* She ran to the restroom to look in the mirror. Turning to the left and then the right to catch her reflection from all sides, she couldn't tear herself away.

Oops. She checked her watch and realized that she was almost late for clocking in for her shift, so she shoved her things into her locker and smoothed her clothes. For the next hour, she tried to focus on her job, but every time she passed a mirror on the sales floor, she paused to look at herself, beaming with pride. Nothing could dampen her mood. Until *they* came in.

Molly had been struggling to get a cute new dress onto a mannequin when she heard activity behind her and looked to see if a customer had come in the store. Her heart sank to see Kim, Pam, Marcy, and Jade headed right for the expensive jeans. She'd have to help them and treat them like every other customer, or Donna and Amy would know something was up. Molly helped them into a fitting room, hoping they would take their time rooms so Donna would be gone before it was time to ring them up. Trying to drag out the length of their stay, Molly kept bringing them new styles and different options after they had tried on everything they had picked out themselves. Good deflection disguised as great customer service.

Phew! Donna left before the girls had finished picking out what they wanted to buy. Still, Amy had to be the one who rang them up, because Magna had rules against associates ringing up their own friends or family members. *Not that they're my friends.* Molly poked her head into the stockroom. "Amy, there are some girls from my school here to buy some things. Do you want to ring them up, or should I?"

"I'll come do it. Thanks, Molly." She wiped her mouth with her napkin and stood up.

Kim and Pam were laughing about something while Amy scanned their items. Together their purchase totaled $104.42. Kim took a five-dollar bill out of her purse and handed it to Amy along with their ten Bounty

Bucks. Marcy and Jade were next. Their purchase totaled $138.87, so Jade gave Amy ten Bounty Bucks and two twenties.

Molly wanted to disappear. *Why did I do this?* It really hadn't felt wrong. . . . *Oh come on, even if I hadn't realized the truth of how wrong everything was at first, I could have ended it anytime since then. But now it's too late. Right? Should I do something? I'd get fired, probably.* She stayed busy filling the bag bins and taking the extra hangers to the back room while Amy seemed to go slower and slower. Finally it was over. The girls had their bags, and they were ready to leave. *This is my last chance to put a stop to it. . .but I can't.*

"Okay, bye you guys. See you tomorrow at school." Relieved, she watched Amy closely for the next few minutes. *Did she suspect anything? No, why would she?*

The evening passed quickly, and nothing was said about Kim and the girls. Amy seemed completely normal, and Molly could finally breathe easily. She could move on and not have any of that hanging over her head. *Think about your promotion, not all that other stuff,* she kept telling herself.

By the time Molly left work that evening,

she hardly gave it another thought. She ran into the house after her dad drove her home and shouted up the stairs. "Mom? Can you come down here? I have news!"

"Huh? We drove all the way home together, and you said nothing about any news." Her dad was clearly confused.

"I know! It was so hard to contain myself, but I wanted to wait to tell you both together." Molly grinned.

"What's all the commotion?" Molly's mom pulled the belt tighter on her robe as she entered the kitchen with a rolled-up magazine under her arm.

"Guess what!" Rather than waiting for them to guess, Molly just showed them her name tag.

"I'm guessing that means something good, but what does 'ANLT' mean?" Mr. Jacobs asked, holding the tag at arm's length and squinting.

Molly's mom took the name tag from him. "If you'd wear your glasses. . ." She sighed. "AMIT, it says AMIT," she told her husband. "What does that mean, Molly?"

By the time Molly got done explaining the details of her promotion and all that Donna had said, her parents were grinning widely.

"I'm so proud of you, sweetie," Dad said.

Her mom gave her a hug. "Congratulations, Moll. Those people sure think highly of you. Keep up the good work."

Ugh. They do think highly of me. Molly's stomach flipped as the image of Kim handing over the Bounty Bucks flashed through her mind. *Nope, not going to go there.* She shook her head to clear her thoughts. "Thanks, you guys. Now, I have some homework to do. I'm still working on bringing up that biology grade after that test I bombed."

"That sounds like a great plan—we'd hate to see you have to quit after such a great accomplishment. Off you go!" Her mom waved her magazine toward the stairs.

"A rolling stone gathers no moss!" Her dad called up the stairs.

Molly and her mom both groaned.

Molly slipped her corduroy jacket on over her lace-trimmed tank top and pulled on knee-high leather boots. *Wow. That's a long way from my usual T-shirt, jeans, and running shoes.* She ran some smoothing serum through her thick hair, hoping to tame the flyaways, and then swiped some gloss across her lips. She bent down to grab her book bag on the way out of her room.

Flanked by Sara and Jess, each wearing a screen-print tee and jeans, she walked into school a little while later. She felt like a million bucks. *Thud.* Her heart sank when she saw Kim and Jade leaning against the wall near the girls' restroom. They had on some of their new clothes and just stood there watching her. They didn't smile, nod, or say a single word. *Creepy. I'm going to have to keep my eye on them. If only I could go back.*

Jess must have seen her watching them. "Don't mind them. What could they do to you anyway?"

Molly groaned. "They could get me fired. They could threaten to get me fired so I would give them more stuff. They could get me into trouble here at school by spreading rumors. . . . Oh, there's a lot they could do."

"I wish we'd been a lot smarter and told you not to get mixed up with them," Jess lamented.

"Tell me about it. Too late now, though." Molly sighed. She was stuck.

"Yeah. They're trouble. Just steer clear of them. Maybe they'll leave you alone now." Sara brightened.

"Ever the optimist, Sara." Molly chuckled.

"Oh well. What's done is done. I can't worry about it. I'll have to deal with whatever else they do as it comes up. I'll just pray they stay far away."

Chapter 8

→

ALL FOR ONE

Oh, my bed. Approaching the church Sunday morning, Molly longed to be back home rolling around in her covers. Even the appearance of the church annoyed her unless she was going there for youth group. Stained glass windows on every side, deep mahogany wood floors and walls, beams on the ceiling, an organ with floor-to-ceiling pipes that the organist sure wasn't afraid to use, a choir of one hundred people in gold robes. The whole thing was all very regal and rich, which, to Molly, meant stodgy and impersonal. Least favorite to her were the long, entrapping, purple-velvet padded pews. She shuddered just thinking of sitting in one of those coffins.

She thought back over some of the churches

she had visited last summer when they did a local missions trip visiting various area churches to help them with service projects. Some of those churches were nowhere near as stately but were far more personal. She felt closer to God amid the casual spirits of the people who encouraged individuality and freedom of expression than amid hymns and repetitious prayers.

Molly looked at her mom and dad in their Sunday best—Mom in a dress with pantyhose on and Dad in a suit and tie. They thrived on the traditions and constantly argued that no contemporary song could even come close to the majesty of an old hymn. Perhaps they were right—if majestic music was what you were looking for. Maybe she didn't know what she was looking for, exactly.

Molly sidled into one of the pews with her parents beside her on the right. She tried to scoot all the way to the other end so she'd have an escape route, but another family had begun to file in on her left, each person like another nail hammering her into a velvet coffin. Fidgeting, Molly hoped she wouldn't have to excuse herself to go to the restroom.

Think about something else. *Count the hats.*

One, two, three. . . Did that woman have feathers and a veil on her hat? Molly rolled her eyes. Finally the organ started to play—its opening notes so loud that everyone jumped.

Molly giggled.

Mom ground the heel of her shoe into Molly's foot.

"Ouch!"

"Behave yourself," she hissed at Molly, turning red as people looked at them.

"Sorry." Molly turned her attention to the song leader. She opened her hymnbook even though she knew the song by heart. "Blessed assurance, Jesus is mine. . . ."

After the customary prayer, song, communion, prayer, song, offering, prayer, Pastor Marshall took his place at the podium. "Before I get started on my sermon, which will focus on. . ."

Sigh. Molly tried to contain her frustration. *He's going to do something even before he preaches. I'll be stuck in this pew all day. Now I really have to go to the bathroom.* She looked down each side of the pew. Her choices were to step over five adults on one side or two adults, two kids, and a lady with a walker on the other. *Stuck.*

". . .we have an announcement to make. I'm

going to let Pastor Mike tell you what's going on." Molly sat up a little straighter and forgot about needing to go to the bathroom. Curious, she even put down her bulletin to listen.

The youth pastor looked out over the families and smiled at some of his young people. "Folks, this announcement is a long time coming, and we're so glad that it's finally here. Beginning next Sunday, in the fellowship hall, we're going to begin holding a teen worship service. We feel—" He was interrupted by cheers as his words sank in. After giving the youth some time to celebrate, he smiled and continued. "We feel that our youth need something a little different. They need to be reached in ways that speak to them where they are."

He made eye contact with several adults in the congregation. "Now, I know that many of you feel that they should be raised in the same traditions and with respect for the history of the church. I agree with you on one level, but we're not willing to sacrifice their church involvement and spiritual growth just so we can be sure they know the hymns the same way their parents do."

He held up his hands in front of him, asking everyone to hold on. "But even though there will be some changes, important things will continue. They'll just have a different flavor. There will be a time of contemporary worship rather than hymns. There will be communion time, but the music played and the format might be a bit different. There will be an offering, but it may be done as a contest or a game sometimes. The youth will be taught to tithe, but the teaching methods will be different."

I can't believe it. Molly looked around for some of her friends. She saw Sue sitting across the room. As a youth leader, Sue surely had something to do with making this happen. And across the aisle from Sue, Molly could see Brad's tall head next to. . . *Wait a second. . .Sara? It can't be.* Brad leaned forward to pick something up, and Molly got a clear view of Sara, who just happened to turn at that very second and lock eyes with Molly. They both grinned. *Wow! It's a good day.*

The senior pastor took the podium again. "I hope you can all see that we aren't separating like this because we can't cooperate. We're doing it as a celebration of the different needs in our body. We aren't doing it as a concession to the irreverence of youth. We're doing it out of the realization that we're missing out on meeting a huge need in this body." He looked out and made eye contact with several members. "Mark my words, in ninety days I'll be able to report that the Sunday morning attendance of our teens has doubled. We can't reach them if they aren't here. And even though some of them are technically here, they aren't being reached."

Oh boy. Some people aren't going to like this one bit.

"One thing I want to caution the young people on, though, is to hold fast to the teachings and traditions of those who've come before you. They're rich and meaningful. Someday you'll be grateful to know 'The Old Rugged Cross,' 'Amazing Grace,' and 'It Is Well with My Soul.' Don't forsake your roots for what is new and fleeting. In all things may we all be open to the leading of the Holy Spirit and willing to move where He leads."

The entire congregation broke out in spontaneous applause and got to their feet— every single person. Molly looked on in awe. Something was finally being changed for the better.

The pastor moved into his sermon for the day, but Molly couldn't stop thinking about the very first youth service that would take place in just one week. Now to figure out how to get Jess to come.

"Hmm, I don't know. I guess I have mixed feelings about it." Molly's dad hesitated as he turned the key in the ignition.

"Well, I think it's fantastic." Mom nodded vigorously. "If you want my opinion, this should have been done a long time ago. The Wednesday night youth group is more about fun than Bible teaching. Sure, there are devotions and a little bit of teaching, but I think we've missed out on some real opportunities with our young people. They need to learn the Bible and be held to higher standards of living."

"Well, sure. But doesn't that happen on Sunday mornings?" Dad countered. "Pastor Marshall teaches the Bible."

Molly looked out the window, trying to disappear into the landscape.

"That's the whole point, John." Mom flipped her sun visor down hard. She took a deep breath. "They don't relate to the adult teaching. It doesn't reach them where they are in their lives."

"Well, that's only a problem because we as a society have taught them that it's all about them. We have to cater to young people instead of having them learn from us. Whatever happened to 'children should be seen and not heard'?"

That's it. Molly whipped her head around. "Dad! Seriously? Let me ask you this. . . . When you train people at work, do you train them all the exact same way or do you figure out how to reach everyone differently and how each individual is best motivated according to what will achieve the most results?" Molly waited confidently.

"You know the answer to that, because I've explained it to you before, Moll." His knuckles were white on the steering wheel as he looked up at the roof of the car and collected his thoughts. "You know what? You're one smart cookie."

Molly wiggled her eyebrows and grinned with victory. She offered a concession by throwing him one of his beloved clichés. "Chip off the old block."

Chapter 9

SHALL WE DANCE?

Monday morning magic awaited Molly, Sara, and Jess when they entered the school. Festive posters lined the hallways, and the doors were brightly wrapped like Christmas packages with shiny paper and bows. Glittery stars and sparkly icicles hung from the drop ceilings in classrooms. Teachers had their bulletin boards and windows decorated with die-cut Christmas trees and ornaments. Holiday music softly played on the PA system.

"I think they're trying to get us in the holiday spirit, wouldn't you say?" Sara gestured down the hallway strung with blinking colored lights.

"I don't remember them getting this decked

out before. Do you guys?" Molly turned in a full circle as she gazed at the decorations.

Before they could answer, the music stopped and the system squawked and squealed as someone got ready to speak into the microphone. "I think we're about to find out what's going on." Jess pointed up at the speaker on the wall.

Students collectively froze in place and looked up at the ceiling.

"Good morning, students," the principal's voice chirped. "On behalf of the faculty of Ford High School, we want to welcome you to Winter Wonderland! Enjoy the holiday decorations, and let them put you in the mood for our Winter Wonderland Dance Festival that's only two weeks away. I hope you're making your plans, getting your tickets, and shining up your shoes. It's going to be the best party this school has seen—ever! And I have the distinct privilege of announcing to you that there will be a live band. Does anyone know of a band called HiJinx?"

Cheers erupted throughout the school, and the principal had to wait a full minute before he could resume his speech.

"I'm so glad you're excited. We all are! I can't

wait to see you there. It's going to be something to remember. Merry Christmas, everyone." The microphone squealed again as it switched back to the Christmas track.

"So, you guys going to the dance?" Molly asked Jess and Sara as they started toward their classes again.

"I'm going to go." Sara blushed.

"Oh, I'm sure you're going." Jess laughed. "You and Brad have been joined at the hip for weeks now."

"How about you, Jess? You going?" Sara asked.

"I. . .well. . .I. . .I'm not sure," Jess said evasively.

"Whoa! Are you holding out on us? What's the story?" Molly pulled Jess to a stop right in the middle of the hallway.

"It's just that I might—I said *might*—be going with Todd Stotter. We've. . .um. . .well. . . we've been talking a little." Jess blushed beet red.

"Really? Wow. I can't believe you didn't tell us about that." Molly was shocked, and Sara just stared. Jess with a guy? *I didn't see that coming.* She just seemed too independent and self-assured. Who'd have guessed?

Molly decided to be up front with her

friends, too. "I'm going to ask someone to take me. Is that too weird?"

"Who? Who?" Sara jiggled impatiently from one foot to the other.

"No, it's not weird at all. Good for you." Jess looked impressed. "Who is it?"

"His name is Matt. He's the brother of one of the girls I work with. He goes to St. Augustine. Christa said he doesn't have a girlfriend right now. He's a junior, though. He may not be interested, but he's super cute. So, I'm going to give it a shot." She shrugged.

"Wow. You've really changed." Sara looked impressed. "The old Molly would never have had the nerve to do that."

The bell rang to signal the start of first period, and the girls turned to go their separate ways. "When are you going to do it?" Jess called down the hallway.

"After school today." Molly yelled back. "Wish me luck."

Jess and Sara both gave her a thumbs-up. "We're coming over!" Jess shouted.

Molly just laughed and shook her head.
How did I know she would say that?

After school they giggled their way into the Jacobs house. It seemed like Jess and Sara were as panicked about the phone call as Molly. "What are you two so uptight about? You don't have to talk to him!"

"We're just nervous for you," Sara said with grave sympathy. "I couldn't imagine doing what you're about to do."

"Well quit it! You're making it worse." Molly flopped back on her bed and covered her eyes with her hands.

"Is your mom home?" Jess asked wisely. She would have a problem with Molly calling a boy and asking him to take her to a dance.

"No, she's out at a book club meeting or something."

"Okay, so quit stalling. Let's get this thing over with." Jess held out the phone.

"Okay, okay." Looking at a scrap of paper she had wadded up in the front pocket of her jeans, Molly sat on the side of her bed with the cordless phone in her hand. She read the number a few times and wiped her sweaty palms on her jeans. Her lips moved rapidly as she rehearsed what she wanted to say.

It's now or never. Molly punched in the numbers in as fast as she could and then held the receiver to her ear. She took several deep breaths while it rang. "Hello. May I speak to

Matt, please?" She nervously shook her hand and crossed her fingers while she waited.

"Hi, Matt. This is Molly. I work with Christa at Magna. We've met a few—"

"Hi, Molly. How's it going?"

"Oh, you remember me? Great." She gave Jess and Sara a thumbs-up and then winced. *Why did I tell him I didn't expect to be remembered?*

They grinned and nodded.

"Well, the reason I'm calling is that my school has a big Christmas dance in a couple of weeks. HiJinx is the band that will be playing—can you believe that?"

"Yeah, I heard that at school today. Word travels fast." He laughed.

"It's going to be great. . . ." She hesitated, afraid to ask the big question. Jess nudged her thigh and gave her a nod of encouragement.

"Well, I was wondering if you'd like to go to that dance with me." There. It was over. She'd done her part. Now she just mentally begged him to say yes.

"That sounds great, Molly. I'd love to."

"Really? Great! I'm sure we'll have a fun time. Okay, I'll be in touch as soon as I have more details. It's the third Saturday this month—the nineteenth."

"I'll be looking forward to it. Oh, hey, let me know what color your dress will be, too. Okay?"

"Okay, Matt. Thanks. I'll talk to you later." She hung up the phone, collapsed on the bed, and heaved an exhausted sigh. Then she started to giggle. "I. . .can't. . .believe. . .I. . .did. . .that!" She sputtered out through her nervous laughter.

"I'm totally impressed." Jess smiled at Sara and nodded.

When Molly recovered, Sara said, "Now that we all have dates, we have to figure out what we're going to wear."

"Ugh, I know! Matt told me to let him know what color dress I chose—probably so he could get me a matching flower."

"Oh, that's really sweet!" Sara made a fist over her heart and swooned.

"Yeah, but I have no idea what I'm going to wear. I have a little money saved, but I've been spending so much on casual clothes for work that I don't have much. I could ask my mom and dad, but they'll put up a fight about spending a lot of money on a dress that I'll only wear once. It would be different if it were prom or something."

Jess shook her head. "Well, I can guarantee that my parents can't help me buy a dress, so

I won't even bring it up to them. I'll have to borrow one from someone or wear something I've got." She looked thoughtful. "Unless I can figure out a way to earn some money."

Molly's eyes brightened. "I have these two dresses from my cousins' weddings you could see if either of you can wear them. They don't, um, fit me on top anymore. And there's no room to let them out."

"Your dresses will be way too short on me, Moll." Jess walked to the mirror, held one of the dresses up to her shoulders, and shook her head.

"This one might work." Molly held up a dusty mint green dress with layers of organza that cascaded into a slight train in the back.

"I'll try it on. . .but. . ." Jess looked skeptical. She pulled it over her head and adjusted it on her tall frame.

Molly and Sara sputtered behind their laughter. It was way too short, and the torso looked all wrong on Jess. The color beautifully set off her sea green eyes, though. "We could have it altered," Molly offered.

"Thanks, Moll. But with all of these layers of fabric and the delicate beadwork, it would cost a fortune to alter this dress. I might as well buy a new one."

The second dress was iridescent burgundy with swirls of plum and rich ruby throughout. It would be perfect for the Christmas dance and would look just right with Sara's long, wavy dark hair; pale, luminescent skin; and blue eyes.

"Oh, wow! That one is gorgeous. But, yeah, they're both mermaid-style which will never work over my saddlebags, even if I could get them on." Sara patted her hips and turned sideways to look in the full-length mirror on the back of Molly's door. She didn't even bother trying them on.

Molly went back to her closet and took out a half-gallon glass jar full of coins and dollar bills. She dumped it out on the bed. "Let's see how much money I have. I'll share it with you guys if it helps." They counted it all out across the bed in little piles of ten dollars each: $112.77. "It's not bad, but I'm going to have to keep out money for the dance tickets. I invited him, after all. That's twenty-five dollars a couple. I do have shoes I can wear, though."

"Oh, I do, too; I just remembered," Sara said. "I have those silver strappy heels that would work with just about any dress."

"Have an extra pair of size nines lying around anywhere?" Jess lifted her foot in the air.

"Okay, so, eighty-seven dollars needs to buy three dresses and a pair of shoes? Do you think I'll have to pay for dinner, too?"

"He'll probably pay, but you should probably have money just in case. So, you should hang on to another twenty-five dollars." Jess moved fifty dollars off to the side. "That leaves sixty-two dollars for three dresses and a pair of shoes. It's not looking good, girls."

Molly fingered the little ribbon bows on her comforter and then paced the room a few times before sitting at her desk. Maybe they just shouldn't go.

Sara tapped her fingernails on the nightstand while Jess thumbed through the pages of a fashion magazine on the bed.

Finally Molly got tired of worrying about it. "Let's go get a snack."

At that same moment Jess put down her magazine and said, "I have an idea."

The snack could wait. "What, Jess?"

"Tell us!" Sara immediately stopped her tapping.

"Well," Jess sat up, dragging her words out. "You know how clothing stores loan out dresses for fashion shows?" She waited for an answer.

Sara just nodded, and Molly said, "Yeah,

Magna does that all the time."

"Okay, now just hear me all the way out, okay?"

Both girls nodded.

"What if we 'borrow' "—Jess wiggled her fingers in the air like quotes—"some dresses from Magna, don't remove the tags or anything, wear them for the dance, and then return them right after it's over?"

Molly was immediately shaking her head in protest before Jess even finished speaking, Sara looked horrified, but Jess held up her hand. "Hold on, I'm not finished yet."

They both closed their mouths. Molly crossed her arms and cocked her head to one side. *I'm not liking this one bit.*

Jess continued, seemingly unfazed. "It wouldn't be stealing because we'd be returning the dresses right away, and you do work there, Molly. I mean, they loan out dresses to people all the time. How much more do you deserve it than perfect strangers to the company?"

"First of all, it most certainly would be stealing, Jess. We can't be sure that we would be able to return the dresses unharmed. Plus, if we got caught, it would be me who lost my job, not you guys. And, yes, they loan out dresses all the time but by their choice and for marketing reasons, not just so someone can wear a dress for free."

"Hold on, Moll. You know, it's not the worst idea I've ever heard." Sara sat up straight on the bed.

"You've got to be kidding me. You're actually considering this?"

Jess got more excited. "Yes, Sara. It's not a bad idea, is it? And it technically isn't stealing, is it?"

"No, it's really not. We'd have to be so careful with the dresses, though." Sara tapped her chin like she was seriously thinking it through.

I can't believe this.

"How would we get them out of the store?" Sara sat forward eagerly.

"We wouldn't!" Molly punctuated her point by getting to her feet so fast her desk chair almost toppled over. "You guys, this just won't work!"

"Okay, picture this." Jess tried another angle. "It's your shift. It's the Thursday night before the dance, and it's really slow in the store. Amy takes her dinner break, so you're alone in the store. With me so far?"

"I'm with you, but I don't want to be." Molly sighed.

"Okay, while Amy's gone, we come in and grab the dresses that we picked out ahead of time. You'll have the security tags removed already. We go into a fitting room and put them in a big shopping bag that we carried in with us. We come out of the fitting room and leave the store before Amy comes back." Jess leaned forward. "Then, after the dance, we come back on Monday night while you're working and do the same thing—only this time, when we leave, we just leave the dresses hanging there for you to put away before Amy gets back. It can't fail."

Jess, likely encouraged by Molly's softened expression, continued. "Then, Moll, we'd all have great dresses for our pictures and for our dates. We all want to look special, don't we?"

"What would we tell our parents, though? I mean, won't they wonder where we got our dresses?" Sara wondered.

"Hmm, good point." Molly pointed her finger at Sara.

"Well, we could just tell them that we borrowed them," Jess suggested. "I mean, our parents don't really talk to each other. You say you borrowed from me, I'll say I borrowed from Molly. . . . Get it?"

"Ah! That would work. But what if Molly's boss sees pictures? And what about Christa?"

"Yeah! That's true. What if Christa brings

a picture to work?"

"Well, your boss won't know anything about us. I mean, lots of girls will have dresses from Magna, right? You'll just have to say you borrowed yours, Molly." Jess had all of the answers.

"I can't tell you guys how much guilt I suffered with after the situation with Kim." *But Kim wasn't my friend—Sara and Jess are.* "I don't know. I'm going to have to think about this. Not only could I lose my job, but it's wrong. There are a lot of lies involved. . . . But it sure would be nice to have a great dress." She shook her head. *Why am I considering this?* "I really do want to help you guys out, too. Oh, and I know just the dress for each of us." Molly sighed, not wanting to even consider it but also afraid of disappointing her friends—plus she truly did want a great dress. . .and it wasn't really stealing. . .or was it?

IT'S DECISION TIME!

The time has come to make a decision. Think long and hard about what you would really do if you encountered the exact same circumstances Molly is facing. It's easy to say you'd make the right choice. But are you sure you could stand up to your friends and disappoint them? What if you truly believed you wouldn't get caught and that you'd replace the dresses before anyone found out? Would you consider doing it? Are you sure?

Once you make your decision, turn to the corresponding page to see how it turns out for Molly—and for you.

Turn to page 127 if Molly decides to say no to her friends by refusing to "borrow" the dresses.

Turn to page 158 if Molly decides that she wants a new dress for herself and her friends badly enough to "borrow" them from Magna.

The next three chapters tell the story of what happened to Molly when she decided to do what she knew was right.

Chapter 10

→

JUST SAY NO

Sara and Jess were chattering incessantly. To Molly their voices sounded like the hum of a fan. Caught up in an internal argument, she wasn't listening to them. She rubbed the ribbon on her bedspread between her fingers while she contemplated her next move. What should she do? She didn't want to disappoint them. . .but she wanted to do the right thing. Still embroiled in her inner struggle, she slowly rose from her perch on the bed and went to the mirror over her dresser. She picked up her hairbrush and began to brush her long blond hair. When she finished, she twisted it and wound it into a knot and then clipped it with a tortoiseshell hair clip.

I want to help my friends—I could just take

the dresses for them. . .okay, for us. But why does my stomach hurt whenever I think I might? It's wrong—that's why! Of course I can't do it. . .but I'd like a dress, too. We won't get caught. No! Don't be silly. You know you're not going to do it. . . .

Lord, forgive me for even thinking of it. Come to think of it, please forgive me for all of my sins along the way that led me to this point. Please help me be a better example from now on. Amen.

Jess's reflection looked at her curiously in the mirror. She watched Molly silently fix her hair. "Hey, what gives, Moll? What's wrong?"

Molly looked Jess in the eye, knowing what she had to say but not wanting to say it. *I have to tell her.* No matter what, she had to hear it now. "I can't do it."

"What do you mean? You want to do it a different way?"

"No, I mean I can't do it at all." Molly shook her head and looked away. "I'm not going to steal from work."

Sara stopped digging in the closet and whipped around to face Molly. "But it wouldn't be stealing at all. Nothing would happen. It's almost impossible for you to get caught."

"Maybe I wouldn't get caught, but I could. And it's wrong, not to mention illegal."

"You're saying you won't help us then?" Jess demanded.

"No, I'll help you in any way that I can. But I can't help you *this* way." She threw her hands up in the air. "Look, you guys are welcome to anything I've got. You can wear my dresses, you can use any money I have. . .anything. But I won't steal for you."

"Molly." Jess looked at her pointedly. "You've already shared your discount with us, which is against the rules. You've also stolen coupons to give to Kim and those girls. You've already done illegal things—things that would cost you your job if they got discovered."

"Are you threatening me?" Molly couldn't believe what she was hearing.

"No no. Not at all. I'm just reminding you that you're not completely innocent in this whole thing. You're already in too deep to back out now." Jess looked at her without blinking.

"No, I'm really not, Jess. No matter how you see my past actions, I'm going no further. I'm out." Molly stared her down.

"Well, we see how we rank in importance to you. We're just not popular like Kim and company. We don't have anything to offer you, so you're not going to—"

Molly interrupted her. "That's just ridiculous, and you know it, Jess."

But Jess continued as though Molly hadn't spoken. "Oh, and thanks for the tips about the fitting rooms not having cameras and when the best time to 'borrow' something would be," she snidely remarked and then smirked at Sara. "Come on, Sara. We have planning to do."

Jess and Sara silently gathered their things and left the room before Molly recovered from her shock.

Molly sank onto her bed—stunned, alone. She couldn't believe that they would threaten her, dangle trouble like that in front of her face, and then use her own words against her. She'd thought they were really her friends. *I guess I was wrong.* She lay back on her bed and grabbed her favorite pillow to squeeze. Her tears mingled on her cheeks like her thoughts jumbled in her mind. Why couldn't she just go back a couple of months and start over?

"Molly, dinner!" Mom called from downstairs.

Rubbing her eyes, Molly sat up, surprised. How long had she been sleeping? She glanced at the clock. *Two hours?* She rushed down the stairs for dinner, blinking her eyes as she went.

"Hey, sweetie." Her mom welcomed her and then looked a little closer. "Have you been up there napping? I assumed you were doing homework after the girls left."

"I guess I did doze off for a little while." Best not to say how long she'd been out cold, or her mom would think she was sick.

"Well, wake up, sleepyhead, it's time for dinner." She smoothed Molly's hair.

"I'm so hungry, I could eat a horse." Dad rubbed his belly as he entered the kitchen.

Molly rolled her eyes and chuckled. "Let's feed the cliché king before he gets going with those things."

Quiet during dinner, Molly was glad her dad had a lot of things going on at work that he wanted to talk about.

Finally, toward the end of the meal, the clinking of the silverware amid the noticeable silence must have become too much for Mom to ignore. "Molly, what's going on with you tonight?"

"Nothing. Really."

Her mom wasn't buying it. She raised her eyebrows and just waited.

"Well, the girls and I just had a little argument. Nothing major. I'm sorry if I've been

131

too quiet. Maybe I'm still trying to wake up. I hope I'm not getting sick." She tried to keep her parents' attention off the argument.

Mom walked around the table, pushed Molly's blond hair out of the way, and felt her forehead with the back of her hand. "You might be a little warm, actually. Maybe you should take something and go back to bed."

Phew. "Good idea, Mom. I'll help you clean up, and then I'll do that."

"Nope. I'll help her," Dad offered. "You skedaddle. We don't need you feeling under the weather with finals this week."

"Okay, then. Thanks, Dad. I'm going to get into bed and study until I fall asleep again. I love you guys."

She walked alone to her classes all the next day. Thankfully she didn't share any with Jess or Sara. *Weird. Just days ago I wished for the opposite.* Rather than eating lunch conspicuously alone, Molly sat in the library—she wasn't hungry anyway.

As she entered her last class, she saw her friends for the first time that day. They were at the end of the hall talking to Kim, of all people.

Why her? What could they be talking about? When they saw her, all three of them started to laugh. *Oh boy.* What had she gotten herself into? *And Jess and Sara? Who are they anyway? Not who I thought they were, that's for sure.*

After a lonely bus ride, Molly looked ahead through the long parking lot to the mall. She still had a ways to walk. Shivering, she pulled the collar of her jacket up tighter around her neck. Maybe she really was getting sick. But, no, she knew that wasn't the problem Her stomach did somersaults as she walked into Magna and headed for the counter.

"Donna, we need to talk."

Donna looked up from the cash register, where she counted out the bank deposit. She used her hip to slowly push the drawer closed until it clicked, keeping her eyes on Molly. "Okay." She had a question in her eyes. "Do you want to go to my office?"

Molly nodded, her eyes welling up with tears.

"What's going on, hon?" Donna sat on the edge of her desk and put her hand on Molly's shoulder.

Looking at everything in the room except Donna, Molly said, "I have to tell you

133

something, and then you'll probably fire me."
She couldn't hold back the tears any longer.
Donna reached below her desk to find a tissue.
Molly pressed it against her eyes but couldn't
stop the flow.

Donna waited patiently for a minute. Finally
her need to know won out over her patient
support. "What's going on, Molly?" Her tone
had grown more serious.

Slumped in her seat, hardly looking at Donna
at all, Molly spilled the story, leaving out nothing.
She told Donna about sharing her discount—but
made sure to mention that she did wear all the
clothes to work at least twice. She told her about
taking the coupons and giving them to her
friends. She also told her about the scheme they
had considered in which they *borrowed* dresses
for the Christmas dance.

When she had finished pouring the facts of
her story out onto the desk in buckets of tears,
she said, "I'm sure I'm fired." She wiped her eyes
and rubbed her temples as relief set in—the
worst was behind her.

"I've really loved this job, and I really, really
appreciate the opportunity." Molly had nothing
left to say, so she collected her purse and jacket
and stood to leave.

"Hold on a second, Molly. Slow down. Let's talk about this." Donna stood and paced the room for a minute.

Molly timidly sat back down on the edge of her seat, still clutching her purse and jacket in her sweaty fists.

Donna took a deep breath. "Here's the thing. I share my clothes with my friends, too. Even the ones I buy with my discount. You wore them all to work, so I'd say it's borderline acceptable, but the fact that you feel bad about it tells me that you understand the intent of the discount is to dress you, not your friends. I appreciate your honesty and your grasp of that situation."

"Also"—Donna twisted her auburn hair around her finger as she continued to ponder the details out loud—"the plan to borrow the clothes is what brought you here to my office. You didn't do it. Other girls would have convinced themselves to try it, that it wasn't really wrong if they brought them back, and that they wouldn't get caught. Or, at the most, they would have said no and then moved on. I'm not bothered that your friends tried to get you to do it, because your friends aren't my problem. I respect that you stood up to them and said no. I also respect that you're telling me about it when you didn't have to. So those two issues are done and over with as far as I'm concerned."

Molly could tell that Donna needed to sort through her thoughts, so she just sat quietly, squeezing the straps of her purse.

"The one thing that really bothers me is the coupon thing. I understand that you didn't quite grasp how it worked when you first took them. At first you thought they were like coupons in the newspaper, free to people for general use. Is that right?"

Molly nodded. *It sure sounds ridiculous when I say it now. But it's the truth.*

"Your so-called friends understood, though, which was evident in their shock when you offered them the coupons. Then, once they had them, you felt kind of stuck, even after you figured out how the system worked and that it actually was stealing."

Molly nodded while Donna continued to work out all the details. She had it all figured out just right. One thing had led to another, and Molly just sank deeper and deeper into the mire. She thought back to the diving board analogy that Pastor Mike had made. After the first bounce, the momentum helped propel her along until the final bounce sank her.

"I'm not going to fire you. But I will have to write up what happened with the coupons and put that in your file." She peered deeply into Molly's eyes. "I hope you understand that I'm obligated to protect the interests of the company, and if anything came up in the future, your file needs to reflect what happened. Can you understand that?" She waited. Molly wiped her eyes again, and then nodded. "I trust you, Molly—you're like a little sister to me. I must say, it's refreshing to see a young person with an actual conscience. It's rare."

"Donna, there's one more thing that you need to know. It's about what they're still planning to do. . .tomorrow night."

At home later that evening her parents sat on the sofa in front of the fireplace, and Molly sat on the floor with her back to the fire. Even with the hot flames at her back, she shivered from nervousness as she told them the exact same story that she had told Donna.

They listened without saying a word, their coffee growing cold in their hands. Mom spoke first. "Molly, it's hard for me to imagine that all of this was going on in your life and we were unaware. How is this possible? How could you let this happen? You risked your job after they put so much faith in you. You were dishonest and a bad example to your friends."

Dad jumped up from the sofa. "You condoned, supported, and even helped people steal from your own place of business—in fact, *you* stole from a boss who has been so good to you. I mean, I'm very happy that you're telling us now, and I'm so glad that you didn't do it when push came to shove. But it did go much further than I'm comfortable with. I have to wonder if you're telling us now because you're repentant or if you're just afraid that your friends will get caught."

"But Dad. . ."

"Molly, this could have been a lot worse. I think you're aware of that." He held up a hand to silence her. "I think your mom and I are going to need a little time to talk about how we feel about all of this. Like she said, though, we're glad you put a stop to it when you did. And we're glad your boss is so forgiving. I find it hard to believe that she's overlooking the coupon thing, though."

Molly hung her head and slunk up the

stairs to her room. She collapsed on her bed and buried her face into her pillow. She could understand why her parents felt like they did. If only she could get them to understand her situation and believe that she'd truly had a change of heart. *I just wish I could go back to the beginning and do everything differently. A few choices that didn't even seem so bad at the time have amounted to me losing my friends and my reputation with everyone.* Molly couldn't control the flood of tears that continued to press against the dam of her thoughts.

After a few minutes, Molly heard a soft knock at her door. Without getting up, she gave a muffled, "Come in."

The door creaked open, and Molly's parents stepped in hesitantly. "Moll, your mom and I are sorry for our reactions. We responded out of anger and didn't think it through first." Dad sat down on the bed beside her and touched her shoulder hesitantly.

Molly sat up quickly, drawing her legs under her.

"We shouldn't have given you such a hard time. We know that you're going to be faced with all kinds of temptations as you grow up. You'll make some great choices, and some not-so-good ones."

Molly looked down at her hands and picked at her fingernail.

Mom grabbed Molly's chin and forced her to look up. "But the most important thing in all of this is that you know that we love you and that you're free to come to us with all of your concerns, questions, mistakes, and whatever else you might face."

She let go of Molly's chin and walked to the window. "Sometimes, like tonight, we might have too hasty a reaction; that's where we're imperfect. We were just taken by surprise over the fact that all of this was going on and we weren't aware of it—I think that stung our parental pride a bit. But we realize more and more of that will happen as you get older and lead your own life. We're just so glad you felt that you could come to us and that you wanted to."

Me, too.

"Also," Dad interjected, "we're very proud of the decision you made in the face of intense pressure from your friends. Admittedly, there were some bad choices along the way, but eventually you arrived at a fork in the road, saw where you had turned onto the wrong path, and fixed it. The end result is what's important. You know what? Your mom and I don't care about your past. We only care about your future. It doesn't matter where you've been. It only matters where you're going. And it sure seems like you're back on the right path."

Chapter 11

BUSTED

"Thanks so much for coming in tonight. I'm so glad we were able to find exactly what you were looking for. Come again and ask for me. I'd love to help you next time, too." Molly walked around to the customer side of the cash register and tightened the handle of the bag from the sale she had just completed. She continued chatting with her well-dressed customer as she walked with her toward the front of the store. "I'm sure you're going to love. . ."

Jess and Sara walked into the store, clearly being careful not to look in Molly's direction. They wandered around the front of the store for a few minutes, never even glancing at her. They each picked up a few pairs of jeans and

a couple of shirts on hangers, presumably to
try on. Sara carried hers in her hand, and Jess
laid hers across the handles of the extra-large
shopping bag she had with her—exactly as they
had planned.

Molly's heart sank—they were going
through with it. They had arrived when Amy
was on break, they had large bags with them,
and they were collecting several items to take
into the fitting rooms. The only difference in
their plan was that she wasn't a part of it. They
hadn't even spoken to her yet.

She knew she'd done the right thing by
telling Donna about their plans. But Molly
wondered if she should warn them. *Oh my.
What have I gotten myself into?*

"Oh, I'm sorry," Molly told the kind lady she
stood beside. "I was distracted for just a second.
I hope everything works out for you. Come
back and see me, okay?"

After assuring Molly that she definitely
would be back, the customer left. They were
alone in the store.

Sara and Jess had their arms full of the
things they were taking into the fitting room
to try on, including the two dresses they were
planning to "borrow" for the dance. Molly

wondered if they actually still planned to return the dresses or if they had decided to keep them. She bit her bottom lip, trying to figure out a way to stop them from carrying out their plan. She even went to the fitting room door and knocked. "You two doing okay in there? What else can I find for you?" Molly hoped that the attention would dissuade them from their plans.

From the other side of the door, Molly heard giggling and the rustling of a paper sack. She shook her head, knowing exactly what they were doing. Neither Jess nor Sara answered her, so Molly shrugged her shoulders, resigned to the fact that the girls were choosing their own fate. Having done all she could, she went back toward the front so Donna could carry out her plan. She wanted to be as far away from the trouble as possible. Donna would catch the girls, and it would be all Molly's fault. She wished she had warned them in some way because she didn't want them to get into big trouble, but on the other hand, she knew she needed to support her boss and stand up for the right thing. *I think I'm going to throw up.*

Trying to stay out of the way, Molly busied herself at the front of the store straightening and restraightening racks and buttoning shirts.

Suddenly Sara and Jess exited the fitting room with their packages under their arms. They hadn't even bothered to cover the things they were taking. Molly could see the dresses peeking right out of the tops of the bags. *What are they thinking?* Silently, Sara and Jess walked to the front of the store without touching anything.

This is my last chance to stop them. If they leave the store. . . Oh no, it's too late. Molly's heart sank as her two best friends stepped over the threshold into the worst trouble of their lives. Only they didn't know it yet. *Here we go.*

The back of the store erupted into a melee of people and commotion. The security guards busted out of the back room and ran out of the store to confront Sara and Jess as they were walking through the mall toward the exit.

Molly overheard the guards tell Jess that they had seen into their bags from the overhead security cameras and mirrors once they left the fitting rooms. Molly knew—she was the reason Jess and Sara got caught, but it sure helped to think it could have possibly been another reason. She hoped and prayed they would believe the guard and not blame her. But feeling their glares burning a hole in her back, Molly could tell they didn't believe him at all.

Molly remained uninvolved when the security guards took the girls to the back room. She watched as they stepped through the door, and just as the door was about to click shut, Molly caught a glimpse of Sara's tearful eyes as she turned to look pleadingly at her one last time.

They were back there for over an hour before their parents arrived. Sara's mom got there first. She bristled through the store like she'd been called from an important meeting and couldn't be bothered with such an inconvenience. She threw open the stockroom door and said loudly, "What is the meaning of this?" Molly closed her eyes and sighed.

Jess's mom and dad arrived next. Mrs. Stuart cried with her head on her husband's shoulder—she looked so sad. Mr. Stuart was stone-faced and unemotional. Molly shook her head. She said a prayer that Jess's dad would soften and show her the love she needed.

The end of her shift neared. She had to start straightening the store to close it for the night when the unthinkable happened. Molly stooped down to arrange a stack of shirts on a shelf near the floor. She heard people come into store and assumed they were customers. She stood up immediately and turned to greet them. Stunned, she stared as two police officers strode right by her as if she weren't even there.

Horrified, she followed them at a distance to the back of the store and then gaped at them as they authoritatively went into the back room. *What are they doing here? Are Sara and Jess under arrest?*

The metal door felt like ice against Molly's ear, but she hoped to hear something through it. She couldn't stand there long, though, because customers came in and she had to help them find things and ring up purchases. Any other time, Molly would have loved her customers, but in her preoccupation, they just grated on her last nerve. *Who cares about your muffin top, lady? Buttons or a zipper? What's the difference? Just buy one!*

Donna came out just before closing time and approached Molly. Sensing her panic, Donna calmly put her arm around Molly's shoulders and squeezed gently. "Here's what's happening, Molly. Magna's policy is to prosecute shoplifters. So they'll be taken to the police station."

Molly stumbled and gripped the countertop with white knuckles to steady herself.

"No Molly, don't get upset. They'll be fine. They haven't done anything in the past—they'll get a slap on the wrist. But this is part of the process, and it will teach them a valuable lesson. Just be glad you weren't in on this." Donna started to walk away but turned around to add, "You know, they had other things in those bags that they were stealing, too. They weren't stopping with just the dresses."

"Really?" Molly slid down the wall to the floor where she put her head in her hands. "I had no idea. I wouldn't have thought they'd have it in them."

"If you'd have asked them a month ago, they probably wouldn't have thought so either."

The house shook with the force of the slammed front door when Molly thundered in after school on Monday.

"What on earth is going on?" Mom ran into the foyer where Molly stood with her back slumped against the door, shoulders heaving with heavy sobs. "What happened, Molly?" She frantically searched her daughter's eyes.

"I'm just so sick of it, Mom. They've completely turned on me!" Molly yelled at the air and punched her fists against the door.

"First of all, young lady, you need to calm down. We'll deal with your problems but not until you can be reasonable. Take a minute to calm down, and then tell me who it is you're talking about." She waited patiently while Molly took some deep, cleansing breaths.

Breathe. Breathe. Breathe. Be calm. Molly clenched her teeth and forced herself to be steady. "They've all turned on me, Mom. Everyone hates me." Her anger had given way to resignation. "Sara and Jess won't speak to me, but they'll sure speak *about* me to anyone who'll listen. Everyone is calling me a rat. Oh, and my personal favorite is Fashion-Police-sta Bible-Thumper. Nice name, huh?"

"Oh dear. That must be really hurtful, honey."

"You have no idea, Mom. I can't take it." Molly took three more deep breaths to fight off the frustration that made her ball up her fists again. "And to make matters worse, Kim and her evil minions have spread the word about me giving them the coupons. So now I look even worse, and everyone is just being so mean!"

"Ah, sure. It's a hard lesson to learn but this is why we, as Christians, need, to avoid even the appearance of wrongdoing. Your choices have hurt your credibility and your Christian witness. No one is perfect, and you're forgiven by God for any sin. But your friends might not show the same mercy. Unfortunately there are consequences to your actions even after forgiveness." Mom gently rubbed Molly's back. "People love when other people fall and especially now, because they probably think that you think you're above them."

"So what can I do about it?"

"Sweetie, I'm going to be perfectly frank with you. You just have to take it. I know you; you can handle it. You aren't the first person to stand up for something righteous, so you aren't the first person to be persecuted without mercy. I want you to think about Jesus. He went through betrayal by His friends to a level you'll never, ever experience. And did He show anger or bitterness?"

Molly shook her head, looking down at the floor. "No, He didn't."

"What did He do, Moll?"

"What do you mean?"

"What did Jesus do in the face of all that hate, ridicule, and even His own murder? What did He do while He hung on that cross?"

Ah. I get it. "He prayed for them. He prayed for His enemies."

"Now you get it. Have you done that, Molly?" Mom didn't wait for an answer. "I think you might be so worried about vindicating yourself that you haven't thought much about what your friends are going through and how they're hurting. Also, you're still a little more worried about how you look in all of this than you are about standing up for what's right. I think you need to consider how you can redirect that passion of yours."

Molly slid to the floor, her back still against the door. She rubbed her eyes, exhausted from fighting her own battle.

"Would you like me to pray with you right now?"

Chapter 12

PASSION RENEWED

"You look beautiful, dear." Mom looked over Molly's shoulder into the oval mirror where she was applying the last of her makeup.

"Thanks, Mom." Molly put down her lipstick and paced the floor of her bedroom while she waited for Matt to pick her up for the dance. Dressed in a beautiful soft plum satin floor-length dress and cute strappy sandals, she had her hair twisted into a knot at the back of her head with a few wispy tendrils loose on the sides. She wore delicate, understated jewelry of little rhinestone flower earrings and a matching necklace.

She closed her bedroom door so she could look at her full-length image in the mirror on the back of the door. She turned to the right and to the left quickly, twirling her dress in dancing motions. Even she had to admit she looked beautiful in her borrowed dress. Molly smiled. In the end, Donna had been so impressed with Molly's choices she decided to loan her the dress she'd been eyeing for weeks. *I guess you can get much further in life by just asking for what you need rather than taking advantage of people in order to get what you want.* She pirouetted in front of the mirror.

The one dark cloud hovering over the evening was that she couldn't share it with her friends. Molly didn't know if they'd be at the dance, and even if they were, they wouldn't want to have anything to do with her. She'd been able to forgive them for everything once she started praying for them. But there was no hope for their friendship until they decided to forgive her, which didn't seem likely because they felt betrayed, too—in a convoluted way.

The doorbell instantly snapped Molly out of her thoughts and forced her back into the moment. Suddenly, at the thought of her first date being let into the foyer, the butterflies in her stomach started fluttering again. She gave herself one last inspection in the mirror and, satisfied with what she saw, crept across the carpeted hallway to the banister where she could look over the foyer. Dad opened the door to a tall, handsome young man who held a delicate wrist corsage in rich eggplant and red. It beautifully coordinated with her soft plum dress, and the rich hues offered her outfit a very wintery feel.

She didn't want to get caught spying, so she said from the second floor, "Hi, Matt."

He looked up and grinned when he saw her. "Hi, Molly." He watched her come down the stairs.

Molly hoped and prayed she wouldn't trip on her new high heels while everyone watched.

"You look great," Matt said when she got to the bottom. "Here, I brought this for you." He slipped the flowers onto her arm and smiled warmly.

"Okay, kids. Before you leave, I think your mom wants to take a picture."

Mom stood to the side, gripping her camera and wiping her eyes.

Molly shook her head and laughed. *Really, Mom!*

Having washed her hands at the sink in the bathroom, Molly flung some of the water droplets into the sink and then reached blindly for a paper towel from the dispenser on the wall while keeping her eyes on her reflection in the mirror. Then she squealed, startled. A second pair of eyes stared back at her from the mirror—and then a third. Jess and Sara had approached her from behind and were looking into the mirror, too. She turned quickly to face them, trembling at the confrontation.

But when she looked into their eyes, her fears melted away. Sara's eyelids were dams holding back the tears, and Jess pleaded for mercy with her big green eyes. Jess spoke first. "Molly, I'm so sorry. I can't believe what we put you through."

Molly gulped and took a deep breath so she wouldn't break down in sobs. Not able to speak, she locked eyes with Jess and nodded.

Sara reached out a hand. "I'm sorry, too, Moll. I would give anything to go back a couple of weeks and erase all of this from our lives. But we can't."

"No, we can't." Molly shook her head sadly. "But maybe we've learned enough from this that it was worth it. It could have been a lot worse."

"Yeah. . ." Jess's voice trailed off. "So, just like that? You don't hate us?"

"Of course I don't hate you. What kind of a friend would I be if I didn't let you learn from your mistakes and move on? This wasn't fun for me, sure. But I love you, and all it takes is an apology for me to let it go."

"No way it's that easy. How can you not hold it against us?"

Sara spoke softly. "Because Molly knows what it means to have really been forgiven. Right, Moll?"

Molly nodded, praying silently that she'd have the right words to say. "That's right, Sara. The Bible says that to whom much is given, much is required. I've been forgiven for my sins—past, present, and future. So I'm required to forgive others for theirs. That even means my enemies. How much more the people I love?"

"I want to know how that feels, Molly," Sara whispered.

"All it takes is asking Jesus to forgive you for your sins, and He will." Molly shrugged. "It *is* just that simple."

Jess shook her head. "I don't know about all of that. But I do know that I want to be more like you, Moll. Maybe I'll check out this church thing you've got going on, after all. But for now, let's dance."

The three friends locked arms and left the ladies' room together, united once again.

The next three chapters tell the story of what happened to Molly when she made the wrong decision and succumbed to peer pressure by stealing clothes for her friends.

Chapter 10

WHAT THEY DON'T KNOW WON'T HURT THEM

Molly made a quick decision, like pulling off a bandage. She'd wind up getting talked into it anyway—Jess could be so persuasive. So she'd get on board now, try to have fun with it, and save them all some time and energy. *It's not like we're actually stealing. And we'll never get caught.*

"I'll do it." Molly paced the room. *What am I thinking? This is so wrong.* The inner voice that wanted to do the right thing screamed at her to stop. But she wasn't going to turn back now. She didn't want to disappoint her friends; plus she really wanted something special to wear for her date. "You guys just have to promise you'll be extra careful and the dresses will go back right away," she begged.

"We promise. We already told you that ten times." Jess jabbed her in the ribs.

"I know, I know. Oh! And you can't wear perfume. And if you use deodorant—which I hope you do—use the spray kind, not the stuff that leaves gunky white streaks on clothes."

Jess and Sara cracked up.

"You've got to relax a little bit, Moll." Jess patted her on the back.

"Yes, please. . .for all our sakes," Sara pleaded with her, still smiling.

"Okay, so let's go over the plan. You're working on Thursday, two days before the dance, right?" Jess confirmed.

"Right. I work five o'clock until close. Amy will take her dinner break between five and six, because that's when we're the slowest."

"Okay, so we'll come in at around five thirty just to make sure Donna is gone for the day and Amy's on break. Sound okay?"

"That's probably the best time. You'll bring the bags?"

"Yeah. I have a couple of great ones. We got them when we bought winter coats, so they're really big and have good handles." Sara popped the top on a can of soda.

"But what if we can't decide on a dress? I mean, we don't want to take up a whole bunch of time in there." Jess looked concerned. "I have a hard time with dresses sometimes."

"Can we go shopping on Wednesday night to get them all picked out?" Sara looked at Molly.

"It'll have to be Tuesday. I won't be able to go on Wednesday. I have church. . . ." *Church. How could she go to church one night and then steal from her workplace the next night? What am I doing? No. No. It isn't actually stealing. It's all going back to the store.*

Molly got to the mall on time on Thursday. But she just couldn't bring herself to go in. She paced outside the main mall entrance for ten minutes. *It's going to be okay. You're not going to get caught. It's no big deal—it's not even stealing.* Finally, at five minutes after five o'clock, Molly went in to work. For the first time in the history of her employment at Magna, she clocked in late. She'd have rather been anywhere that evening than at Magna.

"I'm so sorry I'm late, Donna. I got a little behind trying to get here."

"Well, you just see to it that it never happens

again." Donna eyes twinkled as she teased. "I have to run—dinner plans. Amy's in back. She had to answer the door for the delivery truck. She'll be right out. You guys have a good night." Donna hurried out the door, and Molly was alone in the store.

Nervously she wandered between the racks of clothing, avoiding the dresses like they were rigged with time bombs. She buttoned the front of a jacket, straightened the direction some hangers were facing, fixed the accessories on a couple of mannequins and waited, thankful there weren't any customers to distract her from her thoughts.

The back room door squeaked. "I'm going to take my break since I'm back here already. Do you need anything while my food's heating up?" Amy asked.

"No thanks. I'm fine. See you in about forty-five minutes." *So far, so good.*

Minutes after Amy disappeared and the back door swung shut, Jess and Sara walked into the store. Giggling loudly and bumping into things, Molly assumed they were trying to appear like normal, casual teenagers—but they were going too far. Molly glared at them, shushing them with her eyes—it wouldn't help if they attracted attention of any kind.

"Hi. What are you guys shopping for tonight?" Molly asked, still trying to be normal.

Sara giggled again, which garnered more glares from both Jess and Molly. "Shhh. Come on, you two," Molly hissed at them. "Keep it together, okay?"

Jess and Sara quickly grabbed a few items along with the three dresses they had chosen when they shopped together on Tuesday evening. They took everything into the fitting room and shut the door. From Molly's post on the outside, every noise sounded like it was amplified through the PA system at school. *Amy is going to come running at any moment.*

It's not worth it. They're just dresses. Molly rushed to the fitting room door to put a stop to the whole thing. But at that very second, the door creaked open and Jess and Sara came out carrying their bags—and Amy simultaneously stepped out of the back room from her break. It was almost over, and it was too late to do anything to stop it.

"We've decided not to buy anything." Jess pretended to be a discouraged shopper. "Can we just leave the things we tried on in the fitting room?"

"Of course. No problem." Molly lowered her

voice to a whisper. "Don't forget she knows you guys. Don't try to pretend you don't know me."

They walked right past Amy with their bags of unpurchased merchandise. *Not stolen. Unpurchased. Borrowed.*

Molly noticed with horror that the tags of the dresses were peeking out of the tops of the bags. *Why weren't they more careful? Just keep moving.*

Amy smiled in recognition. "Hey, you guys. How's it going?"

Sara had already wandered away with their bags but turned to wave good-bye to Amy.

"Oh, we're fine. Just out doing some shopping." Jess acted nonchalant and hurried to catch up with Sara.

It was all over. They'd done it—no going back. Molly breathed a sigh of relief that they'd made it out of the store and that they'd all have great dresses to wear to the dance. *But at what cost?* She'd have to get it together. She was a part of this whether she liked it or not.

Amy and Molly stayed pretty busy with steady customers for the next hour. Molly started to relax, and her racing heart slowed to a normal pace. Sometimes she could last minutes without any pangs of guilt. She felt confident

they'd gotten away with the whole thing. . . .
Then it happened.

Molly stood at the cash register ringing
up a customer when she heard a commotion
at the front of the store. She looked up to see
Amy talking to two security guards but thought
nothing of it until she noticed Jess and Sara
standing right beside them. Her heart pounded
so hard she was sure her customer could hear
it thumping. Her hands got sweaty, and her
fingers were trembly and shaky. *Maybe they
won't tell them I was involved.* But they were
her friends, so Amy would probably draw her
own conclusions. *Ugh.* Amy would have to call
Donna. . .her parents. . .the police? The reality
of her trouble pummeled her consciousness.

Like in slow motion, the security guards
steered Amy, Jess, and Sara toward the back of
the store. Jess was stone-faced, but Sara softly
cried and hid her face in the collar of her fleece
jacket. Amy stopped by Molly's side and said
quietly, "I'm going to stay out here on the sales
floor; you go on ahead in the back. They've
already called Donna. She'll be here in a few
minutes." Amy held Molly's gaze for an extra
moment. There was sadness in her eyes.

Molly hesitated at the door to the back

room. Her hand on the handle, she thought about the possibility of still getting out of this. Could it be that Jess and Sara hadn't mentioned her? Would Donna believe she wasn't involved? Could she possibly not stand with her friends and face it with them? Those thoughts swirled around and around in her mind but had no answers to cling to.

Out of the corner of her eye, Molly saw Donna enter the store. As she approached Amy, Molly hurried into the back room. She'd better find out what was happening before Donna questioned her.

Jess and Sara were seated in gray metal folding chairs at the training table where Molly had watched the videos about loss prevention and employee theft. She'd been so horrified that most theft was due to employee dishonesty. Now she was a part of that statistic.

The security guards sat silently on two stools, towering over the girls, glaring at them with their arms crossed on their chests and matching scowls on their faces. Sara was still crying and had wads of used tissues piled in front of her. Jess looked cocky—slumped in her chair, chin raised arrogantly, arms folded. Molly pulled up a chair and sat down beside Jess, whose face was a mirror image of the guards' scowls. No one spoke.

Molly didn't know what had been said about her yet. Could they read her presence there as an admission of guilt? She wondered if she should feign ignorance by asking what was wrong, playing dumb until she knew for sure. *What do I do?* It was too late, though. The door opened, and Donna hurried in, her face white. Her eyes flashed with anger behind the glistening of tears.

She looked at the guards with a question in her eyes but didn't speak.

The guard who seemed to do the most talking stood up from his stool. "We caught these two over by the food court." He gestured toward Sara and Jess. "They were in line to buy food, and I noticed the tags hanging off the clothes in their bags weren't from the stores printed on their bags. When I approached and questioned them, they acted really nervous. We went back to the security office, and I took a look. They had three dresses in there from your store along with some jewelry—"

Jewelry? Molly shot Sara and Jess a questioning look, but neither of them would look at her.

"—but no receipt. She said they had bought them and were bringing them back to exchange but had lost the receipt." He pointed to Jess.

Donna sighed. "No, when I left this afternoon, we had yet to sell a single one of this style." She picked up the beaded powder blue satin dress. "It just came in the other day. I could show you how many came in the shipment, and my records will show that none of them have sold."

The security guard nodded, eyeing Jess. "Does your company have another store locally where she could have gotten it?"

"Well, no. But did she even claim that to be the story?" Donna's sadness faded, and the anger took over. "You see, these three are best friends. Molly is—was—my star sales associate and even a manager trainee. But, like I said, they're best friends. They probably worked together." She turned to Molly, pleading with her eyes for it to not be true. "Is that what happened, Molly? Is it?"

Oh, God. What have I done? Molly gasped for air as her sobs escaped. Her shoulders shook, and she couldn't catch her breath. *Please tell them I'm not involved,* she silently begged her friends. But even if they did, she didn't know if her conscience could handle sitting by while her friends took the fall. *Conscience. What a joke.* She almost laughed at the thought of it giving her a problem after all this. Unable to speak, she just nodded.

"Okay, well, that's that. I'm going to have to call their parents. Girls, please write your parents' names and phone numbers on this slip of paper." The security guard handed Jess a pen and slid a slip of paper toward her. She ignored it. Sara took it and wrote the information for both of them and then handed it to Molly.

"What do you want to see happen here?" the guard asked Donna. "Do you want me to call the police? This is pretty serious. The value of the jewelry and the three dresses is over five hundred dollars judging by the price tags. Two of them would probably be charged with misdemeanor theft, and this one," he gestured to Molly, "would be charged as an accessory. Is that what you want me to do?"

Donna rubbed her eyes with the palms of her hands. Molly noticed she had scrubbed her makeup off and had changed into sweatpants. She must have been sleeping or resting quietly at home—not at all expecting something like this. "I don't think so. If it were anyone else. . . truly. But Molly is special. I have to fire her, clearly—but I'm sorry to do it."

The security guard nodded. "I had a feeling you'd say that. I tell you what, though; if I could, I'd charge just that one over there. She's got an attitude." He shook his head in disgust at Jess's behavior.

"Eh, she's a decent kid, too. She's just scared and trying to act tough." Donna turned and looked at the three girls. "I don't really know what to say to you three. Molly, it's as if you're my own little sister who did something stupid." She shook her head and looked at them for a long time. A single tear coursed down her cheek. "None of you can ever come in this store again, do you understand?"

The three of them nodded, and Molly stared at the ground.

Waiting for her parents to arrive was so hard for Molly. *They're going to kill me. No, worse— they'll be disappointed. Ugh.* What would have happened if Donna had called the police? Molly wanted to talk to her, to say something that would make it all go away, but she remained quiet, sure nothing she had to say would make a bit of difference.

Twenty minutes later—though it seemed like three hours—Sara's mom arrived first.

Minutes later Jess's parents appeared. They
talked with Donna and the security guard
who had stayed in the store to wait with them.
Molly's parents arrived a few minutes later. Mrs.
Jacobs sobbed and leaned on her husband for
support. She shook her head and whispered,
probably praying.

Chapter 11

YOU PLAY, YOU PAY

Out of work, grounded for life, a social outcast at church and school, a disappointment to her parents—Molly realized a little too late that everything she'd worked for could be lost in a moment, in one stupid decision. Back on her bed again, with Rocco stretched out beside her, was the only peaceful place to be in the days since the "incident." Molly hoped she'd be able to fall asleep so the time would pass more quickly.

Her hands linked behind her head, legs stretched out straight in front of her, she seethed. Yes, she *was* mad. Sara and Jess hadn't stuck to the plan. They were supposed to leave the mall right away, not go eat in the food court. And then, they didn't have to let the guard look in their bags. They could have walked right out at that time. The security guards had no power to detain them or search their property. She had told them all that when they were planning. But no, they got ultra-confident and did something stupid that cost them everything. *Ugh! It didn't have to happen this way.*

She jumped off the bed, too frustrated to rest, and paced back and forth across her room. She had nothing at all to do. Finals were over. They were on vacation from school. She wasn't allowed to speak on the phone or use the computer. She no longer had a job. *What do people do who have no life?*

Wandering to the nightstand, she remembered a book she had started a few months ago. She picked it up and opened it to where the bookmark held her page, but it didn't seem familiar at all. She turned back a few pages, trying to refresh her memory about the story. It was no use. She remembered nothing about the book and had no interest in what she read.

Several days blurred into each other until it was finally Christmas Eve. Molly hoped her parents would be able to put all this behind them to celebrate Christmas together, like a real family. That night there would be a big dinner at Molly's aunt's house. *I'll probably be the outcast.*

Molly helped her dad load gifts into the trunk of the car. "Dad, can I ask you a question?"

"Hmm?" He seemed distracted as he rearranged packages in the trunk so more would fit.

"What does everyone know? I mean, the family—Grandma, Aunt Pat, the kids—what do they know about me?"

"We haven't told anyone anything, Molly. It's too much of a shock to us still, and to be honest, your mom and I are too embarrassed. We have always prided ourselves on your ability to make good decisions. It's hard to admit to people how wrong we were." He shut the trunk and went into the house without another word.

Will this ever end? Will I ever be able to put it behind me?

Christmas passed without much fanfare. Molly looked over her room at the presents she'd received. She knew they were given to her reluctantly, bought during a time of celebration—before the bomb went off. She'd been given some cute clothes, some makeup, and a little television for her room she'd been begging for. It still sat in its unopened box, awaiting an unknown date when Molly's punishment was lifted. Somehow it seemed an inappropriate time to celebrate with gifts and new gadgets anyway.

A few days after Christmas, sitting quietly in the front seat on the way to her twice-yearly dentist appointment, Molly picked at invisible lint on her jeans and played with the seat belt strap, wishing something would break the deafening silence. Molly and her mom hardly talked anymore, and Mom's almost-readable thoughts screamed in the awkward silence.

Molly knew her mom was disturbed by the events of the past month just about every waking moment. Though she'd said everything and tried anything she could think of, Molly could do nothing to convince her parents she was truly sorry. She looked in the glove compartment, wishing with all her might to find a fun magazine or some other distraction in there.

Finally she couldn't take it anymore. She turned the radio on to their favorite Christian station. The last few bars of a song were fading as the host welcomed a guest, Penny Summerfield, author of *Handbook of Grace*.

"Hi, Penny. Welcome to the show. We're so glad to have you here with us today. We'd like to offer you a *Penny* for your thoughts." The radio host laughed hysterically at his own joke.

Penny laughed like she found it funny that he thought his joke was original. Molly imagined her saying, "Ha, ha, like I haven't heard that three times since breakfast." But, of course, she didn't.

"Tell us about your latest book, Penny."

"Sure, Phil, *Handbook of Grace* is just that. It's a handbook, a guide, if you will, to help you navigate the path of God's grace and see where it's at work in your life every step of the way. You see, sometimes people—Christians—don't realize that hardships and trials in life can be an act of God meant to steer them more solidly onto the path of His will for them. The roadblocks and speed bumps that He puts in the way are just measures of His grace as He helps guide the way."

Molly didn't think all that she'd been going through was an act of God. He didn't make her steal. *But could He have had something to do with me getting caught? No, that's pretty much all Sara and Jess's fault.*

"Phil," Penny continued, "sometimes we

expect things to go our way all the time, and we get angry when they don't. We can get angry with God, with other people, even with ourselves. But, oftentimes, the hardship is God's answer to a mistake or a wrong turn that we've made. If we're walking outside of His will for us and He uses circumstances to kind of bump us back in line with His plan, why do we not rejoice in that and thank Him for His attentive concern for us? Rather, we get bitter, angry, and resentful of our own mistakes and others who were involved along the way."

"Those are some great points—" Phil started to say.

But she wasn't through. "God's grace is there. It's right before us. Yet we dance around it, step on it now and then, rub it into the ground, ignore it, and turn away from it sometimes. But when we do that, we blame everyone but ourselves. Rather than grabbing the grace of God and applying it to our lives, we shun it and then resent that it wasn't there when we're the ones who pushed it away."

"I hear what you're saying, Penny. But how, exactly, does one, as you said, 'grab the grace of God' and apply it to our lives?"

"Aha! That's the key question right there."

She sounded excited about her subject.

"Well, I can't wait to hear the answer," Phil said emphatically. "Let's take a commercial break, and when we come back, I think we're in for a treat, folks."

Hmm. She's not so bad. Molly was surprised at her interest, but Penny's infectious excitement and the fact that the subject spoke right to Molly's own heart was too much for her to ignore. Mom leaned forward and turned up the radio just a bit and they sat in silence, listening to the commercials.

Molly considered what she'd just heard in light of the events of the past few weeks. Her anger was misplaced. She had no right to be angry with her friends or her boss—she only had herself to blame. She also had no right to resent her punishment or her parents' disappointment. *But I can't help it.*

"We're back with Penny Summerfield, author of *Handbook of Grace.* She's about to tell us how a person can grab hold of God's grace and apply it to his life. I can't wait to hear the answer to this. Penny?"

"Thank you, Phil. Well, I'm sorry to say, there's no formula. As you know, as a Christian yourself, God's grace is free and available to all people. But how do we 'apply' it as I mentioned? Well, grace is freeing, it's the gift of God that gives us the freedom to walk in righteousness. Because of God's grace, we don't have to pay the price for our own sins. Jesus already did that for us. So, we are invited to claim that payment and walk in the freedom not to sin."

"Wait, the freedom *not* to sin? That seems like a strange way to put it."

"Oh, Phil, everyone is going to do wrong— we're fallen beings. But it's only the follower of Christ, through the power of the Holy Spirit, covered in the grace of God, who truly has the freedom and the power to say *no* to unrighteous behavior. We can say no whether it's blatant sin—unholy attitudes like jealousy, pride, selfishness, anger, resentment—or even just being passive and unresponsive to God's call. We have the freedom, through God's grace, to say *yes* to righteousness, *yes* to God's call, *yes* to sound choices and right attitudes of the heart."

Oh boy, I've really been blowing it. Molly sighed.

"Rather than using God's grace as a way out when we sin, let's apply God's grace in such a way that it helps us to say yes to His perfect plan."

"I like what you've had to say, Penny. I hope our listeners are thinking of ways to say yes to God's grace right now."

They pulled into the parking lot of the dentist's office. Mom turned off the car and grabbed her purse from the console between the seats. She looked at Molly and opened her mouth like she had something to say. But, instead, she closed it again and climbed out of the car, shaking her head. Molly took an extra moment to collect her thoughts before she got out.

I had it all wrong. Molly had been missing out on the fullness of a true and right relationship with God. In her mind, up until that point, it had been about staying out of trouble and being forgiven when she did something wrong, rather than running toward the righteousness she'd been called to. She'd been living a battle between the selfish part of her that demanded to be kept happy and the holy part of her that longed to be like Jesus. Which side would win?

Molly and God had some things to work out. She woke up a bit anxious to get to church, hoping she'd find her way back *home*. When she opened her eyes, though, she was immediately taken aback by the brightness that filled the room. It wasn't the yellow of daybreak sunshine. Instead it was a blinding whiteness. Molly jumped out of bed and ran to the window.

Blankets of snow covered everything. Cars were stuck in the street behind Molly's house, and it looked like they wouldn't see the back door again until spring. And the snow still came down in big flakes that wafted down slowly but heavily unto the piles below.

Oh no. There would be no church, and even if services weren't canceled, they'd never make it out of the driveway to get there. *What a bummer.* Molly had really hoped church would be the answer to her innermost needs today. The new youth services had been so wonderful in the weeks since they'd started—she needed to be there.

The snow continued to fall as Molly looked out the window at the beauty that lay before her. *It's just like sin.* Jesus covered sin just like snow covers everything in sight. Suddenly it hit her. *God's not limited to a church building. I don't have to go there to find Him—He's within me. Maybe this snowstorm is part of His plan.* The storm meant Molly had to find her own way back to God—probably just how He wanted it.

The time has come.

Chapter 12

THE TIME HAS COME

"Mom and Dad, I need your help."

They were enjoying the leisure of the surprise snowy morning at home by lingering over a cup of coffee at their cozy kitchen table. Mom had just taken a sip from her pink and white WORLD'S GREATEST MOM mug. She looked up with wide eyes, startled by Molly's emphatic statement. She slowly lowered her cup and swallowed with a loud gulp.

Dad nodded and gestured to an empty chair. "Well, take a seat. What can we help you with?"

"You guys, I've been thinking." Molly paused for a moment, sinking onto the kitchen chair, chewing her bottom lip while she chose her words carefully. "Mom, do you remember that radio show we listened to yesterday in the car?" She waited for her mom to think back.

"Oh, do you mean that author who spoke about God's grace giving us the freedom to live a righteous life?"

"Yeah, that's the one. Well, I've been thinking a lot about some of the things she said and some other things. . . ." Molly took a deep breath. "I think I've had it all wrong."

Molly's parents both leaned forward. "We're listening," Dad said.

"The thing is, I've been angry. I've been mad that I got caught and mad at my friends for doing something dumb enough to get us caught. I've been angry with everyone but myself, when I really have no one to blame but me. Funny how that works, isn't it?"

Molly's mom and dad both nodded but didn't say a word.

"Well, I guess I'd forgotten that being a Christian doesn't just mean looking good to other people. It isn't just about doing as much as you can get away with without getting caught. It isn't about just skating by. It's letting God's grace change your life so that you don't even want to do those dumb things that were once a part of you. Do you know what I'm trying to say?"

Dad sat back in his chair and laced his fingers behind his head. "If I hear you correctly, you're saying that you've been living like a Christian on the outside but hadn't really changed on the inside. So when push came to shove, you didn't have what it took to walk in God's grace and say no to sin. Is that what you're getting at?"

Molly slowly nodded. "Yes, that's exactly what I've been trying to work out in my mind but couldn't quite put it into the right words. Was it obvious to you that I've been living like that?"

Mom smiled. "Honey, you have to understand, we know you very well. We know you love to make people happy. You've always wanted to make your dad and me happy, so you've been a good girl. You've been involved in church. You've done what you're supposed to do. You want to make people at church happy, so you adopted their lifestyles and ways of doing things—you learned how to talk the talk."

Molly nodded along.

Mom took a sip of her coffee and then continued. "You wanted to make your boss happy, so you worked really hard and won her favor and even a promotion. And you wanted to make your friends happy. This time that didn't work out so well for you. But where in all of that do we see that you want to make Jesus happy?"

Molly thought hard about Mom's words. "Mom, Dad, I can't believe I have to say this, but I can honestly say I've never considered pleasing Jesus. Like you just spelled out, everything I've done has been motivated by my desire to satisfy someone else. Most of the times that has been in line with what God would want from me. But you're so right. When push came to shove, I wasn't thinking about Him at all, and it shows by what I did."

Molly shook her head and looked down at the table. *What do I do now?* Suddenly she looked up at them, helpless. "How do I change?"

"Sweetheart." Molly's mom laid her hand over her daughter's hand. "You've made the first step. You've acknowledged you can't do it on your own anymore and you want to live for Jesus, not for everyone else. Now we need to pray together and tell Him. Then your dad and I will help you figure out how to apply it to your life."

"It's like that lady on the radio said, Mom.

Through the grace of God, we have the power and the freedom not to do wrong things to please everyone else. And He gives us the power to say yes to the good things. Right?"

"Exactly. You know, Molly. . ." Her mom hesitated. "I don't think your dad and I have really been great teachers of the love and grace of God."

"Yeah, we've been kind of caught up in the tradition, the religion of it all," Dad admitted. He stood up and walked to the window. "I think your new youth service is just what you needed. What we all needed, maybe."

Molly folded her arms across her chest and grinned.

"I think we're going to start seeing some changes around here."

Lingering outside the store, Molly wasn't sure she should go in. Donna said never to shop there again. But Molly had a different reason for being there. She needed to try to make things right with Donna. Taking a deep breath, Molly shouldered her bag of schoolbooks and walked up to the counter where Donna was doing paperwork.

"Donna?" Molly shifted from one foot to the other.

Donna spun around to see who had approached. She had an inviting smile on her face—she probably assumed it would be a customer—until she saw Molly. Her smile disappeared. "You're not supposed to be here. You're going to have to leave."

"I'm not here to shop. I just wanted to speak with you." Molly's nerve crumbled.

"You don't have anything to say that I want to hear, Molly." Donna looked up at the ceiling as she took a deep breath. She looked Molly right in the eye. "Please leave."

"Okay, I understand." Molly's lip quivered, and her eyes welled up with tears. "I just wanted you to know how sorry I am." She left the store in a hurry and climbed into the car where her mom waited to drive her home. As soon as the door shut, the tears came like a flood.

"She wouldn't listen. . .to. . .me. . .Mom." Molly gulped for air between her sobs.

"Not everyone has a forgiving nature, honey—and most people have limits. I guess Donna reached hers. You're not responsible for whether or not someone grants you forgiveness. Your only job is to seek it. You did the right thing. Now you can let it go and move on."

Molly nodded, but it wasn't enough. "It's hard to let go. I feel like I have so much more to say to Donna. I think I might write her a letter. She can read it someday when she's ready to hear me out."

"I think that's a fantastic idea. In the meantime, be praying for her," Molly's mom suggested.

They turned the corner onto their street and saw two people trudging through the snow from their front porch. *Jess and Sara.* Judging by the footprints, they had come from Jess's house. Molly took a raggedy breath. *Please give me the words, God.*

Once the car stopped in the driveway, Molly hopped out and took a step toward the girls. Her mom went discreetly into the house through the garage.

"Hey." Molly looked away as the snow clung to her eyelashes. "I'm glad you guys are here. Want to come in?"

Sara spoke first. "Is it okay?"

"Does your mom hate us?" Jess asked.

"No, of course not. It's been a little rough around here. But we've worked through everything. I really want to talk to you guys."

Molly impulsively reached out and tugged at their puffy coat sleeves. "Will you please come in?"

"Sure. I'm up for it."

"Me, too." Jess smiled.

They stripped off their snowy coats and gloves in the foyer. Molly said, "You go on up to my room. I'll be right there with some hot cocoa." She could already smell it coming from the kitchen. *Boy, Mom works fast.*

"Thanks, Mom." She took the tray of mugs and cookies. "Please pray for me—for us."

"You'd better believe I will, sweetheart."

Lord, please give me the right words. Help me make a difference.

"You know what?" Molly started right in as soon as she set the tray on the floor of her bedroom in front of Jess and Sara.

They looked at her with huge, imploring eyes and took a sip of their cocoa.

"I really, really don't want to talk about the details of what happened. There's no purpose in it. I want to put it behind us. But I do want to tell you that I'm so sorry."

Jess opened her mouth and raised her eyebrows in shock. "You want to say you're sorry to us? Why?"

"Because I let you guys down. I told you I

was a Christian, but I didn't live it. That's not going to happen anymore."

"Well, we're both sorry for pulling you down. It was all just so wrong." Sara shook her head and shuddered at the memory. "I mean, I didn't like how it turned out. . .but I agree—I don't want to talk about that either."

"I really don't either." Jess shook her head.

"It was wrong. Now let's put it behind us. Okay?" Molly waited for an answer.

"Okay. On one condition." Jess's eyes sparkled.

"What?" Molly laughed—Jess was back to her old self, the schemer.

"I want us all to start going to church together—that youth service sounds cool."

"Deal!" Sara looked excited.

"Now that's the best idea you've ever had, Jess. It's a deal."

My Decision

I, *(include your name here)*, have read the story of Molly Jacobs and have learned from the choices that she made and the consequences that she faced. I promise to think before I act and, in all things, to choose God's will over mine. I promies, before God, to try my hardest to not let the desire for material things, the desire for pleasing friends, or the desire to be popular lead me to sin.

Please pray the following prayer:

Father God, I know that I don't know everything, and I can't possibly have everything under control. Please help me remember the lessons I've learned as I've read this book. Help me to honor my parents and serve You by making right choices and avoiding questionable situations. Please remind me of my desire to please You rather than everyone else. And if I find myself in a tight spot, please help me find a way out and give me the strength to take it. I know that You have everything under control, so I submit to Your will. Amen.

Congratulations on your decision! Please sign this contract signifying your commitment. Have someone you trust, like a parent or a pastor, witness your choice.

_____

Signed

_____

Witnessed by

If you enjoyed

MAGNA

look for more Interactive Fiction for Girls

Book 1: TRUTH OR DARE
ISBN 978-1-60260-399-8

Book 2: ALL THAT GLITTERS
ISBN 978-1-60260-400-1

Book 4: MAKING WAVES
ISBN 978-1-60260-845-0

Available wherever books are sold.